COLONY

DANIEL ERBACH

ISBN

Paperback: 978-1-964963-76-1

Hardback: 978-1-964963-77-8

PART ONE: DUST

Stepping into the de-duster pod, I locked the hatch behind me, got into the cavity, and waited for the second half of the plastic cocoon to close over me. The blast of nitrogen gas from 27 nozzles caused most of the accumulated regolith to spray off my suit, and a vacuum from 27 more nozzles sucked it into the disposal chamber. A second blast and a second vacuum took away more dust. Not done yet. The cocoon opened, and I stepped through the airlock to the next cell, closing the hatch to the first chamber behind me.

When the air pressure stabilized, I unlocked my helmet and set it in a cleansing unit. I backed into a decoupler and unhooked from my air tank, tool carrier, coolant pump, and battery pack. The battery pack powered the exoskeleton servomotors at each body joint, along with the radio, headlights, and power tool battery chargers. I placed them in the unit. Then I got out of my pressure suit and put it in with the rest and hit start. The unit closed and began ionization, followed by high-powered suction of residual dust.

The zoot suit techs would recover the suit, inspect it, pressure-test it, replenish helmet rations (hell-rats to Moonies — we hated them), refill the water bag, empty fecal and urine bags, and disinfect and deodorize the interior. All done per procedure and per contract, for every trip outside. I was wearing only a lightweight body suit with a snug hoodie. It had a Velcro flap in front for my urine tube and one in back for the poop chute. Next, I stepped into the second cocoon, closed my eyes, pinched my nose, and held my breath. I got an air blast and vacuum sequence, sans zoot suit.

Still not done. I stripped off the body suit and tossed it in the bin. The final cleaning step had me stand in a fine mist spray of water with detergent. I washed my face, head, ears, hands, pits, feet, and crotch thoroughly, toweled and air-dried off, and donned a new body suit. Sweet and clean! Ah! Now I was permitted to enter the building. Regolith was brutal stuff — it got into everything, destroyed everything, made everyone sick. It was like gritty, raspy talcum powder. You do not want to breathe this shit. Dust particles under the microscope looked like the sand burrs that got stuck in my socks on my great-grandfather's ranch in New Mexico. It is worse than breathing cement dust. It will make your lungs bleed — popped alveoli. Staying clean was our religion. The Apollo astronauts who walked on the Moon learned this lesson the hard way. They were complete grunge when they returned to Earth.

The other major hazard on the surface of the Moon is cosmic radiation and solar CMEs. The surface gets 200 times the radiation as Earth. During solar storms, we are not allowed outside. Our suits have extra layers of radiation shielding, but this isn't sufficient. When we are on the surface, we work under shield canopies of titanium and aluminum with a copper wire network Faraday cage connected to the ground. The colony modules are covered with huge fly tent-like radiation shields of the same material. The cumulative protection drops our exposure rate down to 4 times Earth's surface. Everyone in the colony wears dosimeters, which are checked every quarter. The Moon is not kind to human beings.

After every trip outside, every worker had to immediately write his after-action report on all activities accomplished — a contract requirement. There was a terminal set up inside the room just for this purpose — no way to avoid it or put it off. It was part of "data gathering." It was also part of the oversight and management evaluation. The third-party QA oversight people read every report and report on our reports. I did my report without grumbling. My pay was high enough to make me tolerate every petty, unnecessary, redundant, bureaucratic requirement. I had paid all my debts during my second deployment, bought a house and truck on my first, and was putting away credit with each new pay period on my third. I wanted lots of land with a log mansion and a sports car and a wife, and kids, in that order. This job made it very realizable. $895,000 a year, minus taxes and benefits (38%), with food, housing, medical, retirement, and transportation all covered. Recreation, home communication, exercise — all covered. It was a sweet deal.

Universal basic income on Earth was $18,000 for every man, woman, and child who did not meet the minimum economic productivity (education level and physical fitness) range. Free housing (very low grade) and free medical and dental (very minimal). About 70% of the world's population was on it. A master's-degreed professional engineer could expect to make no more than $300,000. Jobs for MechE P.E.s were few and far between — lots of competition. This gig was a no-brainer as far as I was concerned, but the Moon was not for the faint-hearted.

I helped to set up and maintain massive mining equipment. The scientists in charge of underground habitats found a very promising subsurface volcanic bubble, 66 kilometers from the colony. Travel each way took 1.9 hours, so I also helped set up the remote man-camp. We were limited by contract to not more than 7 hours outside in our zoot suits, so losing 3.8 hours to travel was not economical for the Company. The mining man-camp would expand into a construction man-camp eventually. I would relocate there once it was up and running — it paid a 10% premium on top of straight hours and OT, due to much more austere conditions. I fantasized about getting a billet for Sharia there, too, but I knew this was a pipedream. She was a farming scientist and had no work at the man-camp, but I could still dream.

Moonquakes were rare and minor in this area. The plan was to build tunnels, carve out the bubble further, install flexible sealant, and start constructing habitats with all the associated support facilities. The bubble was 335 meters below the surface — tunneling to it was taking lots of time, and additional boring machines had been ordered and shipped from Earth at an enormous cost. I got my undergrad degree at the Colorado School of Mining. My master's in mechanical engineering, earned at Western Michigan, coupled with my master welder certification for all metals, made me the perfect candidate for the job of Chief Mining Engineer.

PART TWO: AUDIT

The program was a hundred-year enterprise, begun in 2050. After the United Nations Special Agreement on the Status of the Moon, the Lunar Authority was set up, and a new tax regime was implemented to fund the work. The goal was to set up permanent habitation on the Moon for 1,000 people and to make the colony not only self-sustaining but also economically productive. There were a few technologies that could be enhanced by the lunar environment: pharmaceuticals, electronics, solar power and electrolysis development, farming, fuel creation, biotech, and genetic engineering. But the real draw was tourism, retirement, physical rehabilitation, and medical research. Putting rich sick people and old people on the Moon and making them enjoy it was a high-reward item.

NASA had solved the problem of extreme G-forces' effect on old, sick bodies, getting people into space. It was easier on the human body, with not so much G-force needed to launch from a high-altitude, hypersonic aircraft at 40,000 meters and Mach 8, sending the spacecraft to accelerate into low-Earth orbit. There it would dock with a booster, which would then boost the capsule, again without severe Gs, into a lunar trajectory. Everything is as soft and easy as possible for the geriatric crowd — never more than 2.5 Gs thrust. A dirtside high-rise elevator accelerated at 1.2 Gs.

Landing some four days later, the capsule's passengers would disembark and go through one week of quarantine, indoctrination, and training. Visitors who carried bugs were isolated and shipped back to Earth. Their money was not refunded- they signed a waiver and took a thorough physical exam prior to departure, or no go. No diseases are allowed in our pristine environment. Deployed Moonies went through 2 months of training prior to launching from Earth, and four weeks of training on the Moon. Those of us who worked outside got another 2 months of zoot suit training- much of it in tanks of water, or in Antarctica, or in the Sahara. Tourists went through two weeks of training on Earth, followed by one week of training on the Moon, after which they were shepherded through highly choreographed activities, culminating in the grand highlight of the visit, a 30-minute Moon Walk.

A big part of the one-week training was just learning how to walk in 1/6 G. You do not stride on the Moon- you glide. You lean into it, as if downhill skiing, and you keep your knees very flexed, like in karate practice. It is all in slow motion. If you try to walk like a dirtside newbie, you will literally bounce upwards and lay out backwards. No kangaroo hopping inside the pressurized areas- low ceilings. Leaning in and taking long, gliding strides was the way to go. Few people got hurt (hitting the deck at 1/6 G was pretty tame), and it made for lots of laughs, but most learned.

Including training time, it was a 7-week tourism package. They paid $50 million for the privilege. The cost to the Company was less than one-third of that. They made money. We were up to about 45-50 people per year paying for this fun. So far, we had not killed anyone, and by 2079, 277 people had come and gone. Some were talking seriously about investing in lunar condominiums. It barely dented the cost of the program, but the Company was heavily subsidized, and the prime contract permitted commercial development. This was all pocketed by the Company and did not affect our award fee. The handling of tourists was permitted and paid as an allowable expense if the normal workflow was uninterrupted and normal deployment and R&R schedules were unhindered. The Company made sure this was the case. The Lunar Authority saw tourism as a legitimate business that needed support, just as much as mining or farming.

Tourism and award fees were drummed into our heads. The award fee was tied to specific schedule milestones, the biggest one coming due soon- completing the tunnel to the volcanic bubble. The expansion capacity of the solar farm had an award fee tied to it, back in the day. Getting the electrolysis plant up and running at the specified efficiency was another biggie, as well as the hydroponic farm. There were others: every time we relaunched a lander and it docked in lunar orbit successfully for the trip back to

Earth, we got paid a small fee. Every month, with no lost time accidents, we were paid a little bit of a fee. Every new farm animal born and surviving one month was paid a fee. The list was long.

But the biggest one coming up in the schedule was the tunnel. The tunnel fee was $1.45 billion. A bigger one coming up would be sealing the bubble chamber and testing it with X-ray imagery for microscopic leaks. This paid more fees than all the others — $2.95 billion. Of course, this being a cost-reimbursable contract, we had NO risk. Every nut and bolt was paid by the contract. Every pressure suit, every liter of water, every watt of energy produced, every piece of cake was paid for. Every salary, with all benefits, support, and travel, was paid by the contract. Company accountants and project controls administrators were to be obeyed because they made sure all allowable costs were indeed covered, and this meant crazy amounts of documentation. Our contract profit was 1.375%, but this was a pittance compared with award fees.

They were the CAMs, the control account managers, and they were the high priests and priestesses of the EVMS (Earned Value Management System) religion. EVMS was first introduced by the USN back in the 1950s to track and control nuclear submarine construction. For some contractors, it was viewed as the veritable tool of Satan because it was so pitiless and absolute. But for smart contractors who learned the game, it became a very lucrative game. The

Company was unparalleled in its EVMS performance. The corporate EVMS compliance director owned a mansion on 700 hectares in New Zealand. And an 80-meter yacht. He regularly took cruises to Bali with his buddies and girlfriends.

We had auditors from Earth come up once every quarter for an audit, and the Company made sure they were cared for perfectly, catering to every whim and desire. The male auditors were accompanied by the most beautiful and curvy females on staff (Sharia did a few auditor tours), and the female auditors were accompanied by the most handsome and fit men. Nothing overt was required, but if the auditors could be made a little more cheerful, then this was good for the Company. The escorts (yep, that's what we called 'em) were very professional in manner, and they did their best to be charming and warm. Every one of them was razor-sharp and gave all the right answers. Auditors usually wrapped up their visits with another moonwalk. They could not get enough of them.

PART THREE: THE PLAN

The bubble chamber was 850 meters long, 610 meters deep, and 585 meters wide, shaped like an egg. Its approximate volume, if fully utilized, was over 175 million cubic meters. We would utilize less than half that, so there was plenty of space. It could accommodate our entire staff of 1,003, plus all support facilities, plus labs, farm, storage, recreation—the works. We even had plans for light wells to the surface for farm support, as well as for morale. One of the biggest advantages of living underground is protection from micrometeorites and not-so-micrometeorites. We were repairing punctures to different units of the colony once or twice a month. No big ones came in yet—we had radar to warn us if anything was coming our way. We had hardened inner chambers to protect residents who got there in time. Outer skin patch kits were distributed liberally around the colony. We were re-trained in their use every year (contract requirement). Living underground would also make it easier to deal with the regolith dust. Radiation would no longer be a hazard. Solar storms are eminently survivable when you are protected by billions of tons of lunar rock. We needed to be underground.

There was only one problem with this grand scheme. Heavy lift costs from Earth had been falling for decades, but were still about $250 per kilogram. We would need massive amounts of steel and other metals, machinery, raw materials, lubricants, expendables, epoxy, cement, and tools. It was estimated we would need over three million tons of material. This would cost $750 billion to ship, not to mention the cost of buying and fabricating in the first place—another $750 billion.

Typical launch payloads were 100 tons each, so this meant 30,000 launches. Spread out 30,000 launches over 10 years, and it would require a launch schedule of more than 8 per day, every single day. More realistic was 300 days of launches per year, times 20 years, times 5 launches a day. Still, a very tough schedule to keep. The Company contracted 8 different launch sites around the world to coordinate supplies to the Moon. Every day there were launches from East Siberia, Kazakhstan, French Polynesia, the UAE, China, New Mexico, Florida, and California. All coordinated by A.I. and all very expensive. In the early years of the colony, we had a 9% launch failure rate. Now we never went above 0.4%. One out of every 250 or so had to be aborted and dropped in the ocean—100% loss. Launch insurance was crazy expensive, but fully paid by contract. No risk to the company.

We had 1,003 staff, but would need another 1,000 construction workers, extremely highly trained construction workers, paid ungodly wages, to do the work of fitting out the bubble in a ten-year period (most of us estimated it would take 30-40 years). They needed their own living and support facilities, adding to the launch needs, as well as R&R rotations back to Earth. This was the elephant sitting on the living room floor of the Lunar Colony program. Who pays and how to pay? The engineering was there, the will was there, the volunteers were there. But the costs would run into trillions of dollars. The Lunar Authority, our client, was already making worrisome noises about escalating costs. The money well was not bottomless.

How was the program paid? Blockchain financing—every participating country in the program levied an electronic tax on its citizens—the non-UBI citizens. People on UBI were supported this way but had to give up the right to private housing. They could not own a car. They were limited to government-approved diets. No international travel was permitted if you were on UBI. If anyone wanted to work or emigrate, they had to prove they could make more than $18,000 per year. But they were exempt from the blockchain tax when on UBI. They could spend it any way they wanted, and drugs and alcohol were heavily abused. There were 1.7 billion working people being taxed on average $1,700 per year just to support the program. This paid the cost, but what were the benefits to people on Earth?

The Company knew all this but was scrupulously careful to toe the politically correct line of developing lunar autonomy and economic viability. It was a sham, but a very lucrative sham. All of us knew this too, but we were getting PAID. The Company padded the roster of staff with as many people as they could recruit, train, and deploy. They were paid handsomely for every warm body. The wear and tear on our bodies was not as bad as in zero-G, but still difficult, despite the mandatory 2 hours of workout for everyone, which was monitored and tracked within the HR system and reportable to the Client (award fee for excellent compliance, of course). This was why a gig on the Moon only lasted one year, and we had to take one full year of Earth time to recover before we could return for another stint of low-gravity fun.

Of course, the Grand Master Plan was nothing less than the colonization of Mars, followed by the rest of the Solar System. What a ridiculous joke. We had been working for 29 years to set up and operate the colony, and we still did not have a tunnel to a bubble. We were still a massive money drain on the world economy. The world population had finally stabilized at 9.5 billion people, and most of them were being fed after a fashion. UBI made sure of that. Why exactly did we need to spend $250 per kilogram to lift stuff into space, and spend trillions more to establish toeholds on barren, poisonous moons? The only possible reason to justify it was the extreme pollution on Earth. It was ghastly and pervasive and unhealthy in almost every corner of the globe. Cancer rates went up every year. The plastic-laced, acidified oceans were nearly dead—lots of jellyfish and not much else. The world was getting hotter. The latest, highest temperature for New Mexico was 56 degrees C. Dubai hit 60 eight days out of every summer. In the shade. By comparison, the Lunar Colony was sanitary, healthful, spotless, and pristine. It made no sense to Jeremy Lopez, but I accepted it. I was getting PAID.

One perquisite of working on the Moon was having a girlfriend, or at least a semi-girlfriend. Sharia was a gorgeous Iranian farm expert and botanist, who loved sex, especially sex with me. She was 158 centimeters and 45 kilograms, with a 50-centimeter waist and 97-centimeter bust. The only problem for me was that it was not 7 days a week in all off-hours. She had a life of her own, and she loved to hang out and drink with her girlfriends. When she was horny, I was in heaven. The sex was dirty and rough and wild and fun and exhausting. Then she would kiss me and leave, not to be seen again for 4 or 5 days at a time and not wanting to chat or call. Just like me, she worked long hours. I could try to get another girlfriend, but the pickings were pretty freaking slim. The percentage of females on the Moon was only 27%, and some of them were old enough to be my mother. Most of the attractive women were already shacked up with a boyfriend or girlfriend, so I had to be satisfied with little miss flaming pants from Tehran.

I could not really complain—she was spectacular. Great boobs, great ass, beautiful face, long glossy black hair down to her ass, tight inside. I made sure to NOT whine about anything when she came to me (it was always at my place), but instead to cultivate an air of casual interest—not too clingy, not too uncaring. It was a tough balance. She rarely wanted to talk. When Sharia stopped by, she was a horny devil tearing open my pants. Not much foreplay necessary for her—she just grabbed me and jumped on board. Sex in low-G was damned amazing. It never became stale. We actually did somersaults when we fucked. To be honest, I would not mind some cuddling and kissing and chit-chat afterward, but she rarely stayed longer than 10 minutes after final orgasm. I just didn't get it.

PART FOUR: ICE

In addition to the tunneling project, I was sometimes assigned to the ice miners. My job title was "Chief Mining Engineer," which meant I had to go out and work a lot. You would think that low G was made for long-lived equipment, but you would be wrong. The dust was our eternal nemesis. Also, how do you lubricate in a vacuum? Most oils evaporated in the Sun or turned to sludge in the bitter cold of lunar shade. We used powdered graphite at times; other times it was fine-ground Teflon, with judicious usage of contact cleaner. None of them worked perfectly. Regolith did a number on highly polished surfaces, cutting micro-grooves. Preventative maintenance on equipment took up 40% of our time—no shit. It was tedious and difficult when you wore a zoot suit. Our suits had powered exoskeletons which assisted our hands, wrists, and other joints to work against the inner suit pressure for long work periods, but it was still very, very tough. We had procedure manuals up the ying-yang, with multiple breakdown scenarios that the Moon always managed to expand on.

Nevertheless, the ice miners needed constant support because water is life on the Moon. We had to synthesize our own rocket fuel for return launches to Earth—a contract requirement after our first ten years on the Rock. We always ran low on drinking and washing water. We had to recharge the air systems with oxygen from time to time—this all came from the electrolyzed water. The hydroponic farm needed constant resupply. Waste recycling could never recover 100% of water—it was usually 93-96% efficient. This loss needed replacement.

Moon ice was not nice and clean and provided in big thick veins close to the surface. It was mixed with a lot of lunar trash—gravel, dust, mineral ore—and needed refining, just like any other mineral. It was often hundreds of meters deep. We had to keep it out of the Sun, lest it sublime and evaporate away. The way the Company reacted to ice loss, you'd think they wanted to instill the death penalty.

Out of one ton of ice ore mined, we generally recovered 35-55 kilograms of ice. Pretty pathetic. If we hit a good vein, we could get maybe 110-140 kilograms out of a ton of lunar ice ore. We were lucky when we hit veins because they generally ran for a few thousand meters before playing out. Some veins were 3 or 4 meters wide, but not many. Most were about a half meter wide. The South Pole of the Moon had enormous amounts of ice—it was just too damned deep, spread out, and hard to dig out.

To hit our shift quota of 30 tons of 95% pure ice in a week, we needed to mine 450 to 900 tons of ore, and that is with the refiners working full time. It was grueling work, which is why it paid a premium and why I was out there as much as I could get. We worked 6 x 8-hour shifts by contract, but I could get up to 4 hours

OT for 3 days out of a given week. In order to skirt the 7-hour zoot suit limit, I had to come into shelter for 30 minutes down-time before venturing out again. Twelve hours at time and a half added up. Ice mining was a 24-hour, six-day operation, with Sundays reserved for heavy maintenance.

Thirty tons of ice just met our colony's needs for a week, plus a little. Maintenance was very serious business. I am awfully glad I got that welding cert to augment my Mech. Eng. degree and PE license. I qualified on carbon steel, ductile iron, stainless steel (16 grades), zinc, magnesium, aluminum, bronze, nickel, chromium, vanadium, and titanium. MIG, TIG, stick, and submerged arc were all on my cert card. I was also a qualified welding inspector. I was on my third lunar deployment, and this shit was getting old. I wanted to bank some credit and get the fuck out. Thank God for Sharia! Without her, I would be gnawing the walls.

For whatever psychological reason, the ice miners suffered the highest mental attrition rate on the Moon. Watching a giant, rotating mouth chew through rock for 8 hours a day may be part of the reason. Knowing the entire colony rode on your shoulders was another. When the thing ran right, there was not much to do but watch. I knew some of the guys tossed a monkey wrench into the works to spice up the day, and I didn't mind, because this meant more OT for me.

Fortunately, the rock crushers went down often enough that we did not need to fake anything. We had to avoid showing up on a QC trend chart, so we did not abuse it too much. Statistical process control was not our friend. The QC wienies tracked consumption of carbide teeth, lubricant usage, hydraulics inspections, robotic haul truck breakdowns, bolt torquing, truck tire replacement—the works. Everything, and I mean everything, had to be logged on an hourly basis. The monkey wrench guys could get pretty creative and give the appearance of concern very convincingly. To be honest, I think the Company knew and looked the other way—cost plus, after all. No risk, so long as nobody was caught.

PART FIVE: LAND AND LAUNCH

NASA still used an upgraded version of the SLS to launch the ORION for personnel transport to the Moon. They established a rotation of four people up, four people down on every mission. No pilots were needed- all launches and landings were robotically controlled. For the Moonies we did not get a nice cushy suborbital boost for a tourist vacation. We traveled the old school way, with heavy lift launches and high Gs. To sustain our contractually obligated deployment terms, NASA ran 251 personnel launches per year. This meant that on a turn-around schedule of 12 days per mission, they had to have a fleet of 28 SLS/ORIONs/orbiters/landers (with 7 being back-ups), launching one every day or every other day. On any given day, there were 8-10 spacecraft moving human beings in transit to or from the Moon.

Personnel launches were handled completely separately from cargo launches. It was all NASA, all the time for personnel. The cargo was for the Company geeks to handle. Two of the eight spaceports were shared—Vandenberg and Cape Canaveral—but we had separate launch pads. NASA got priority. They did take a little cargo on the people flights, but it was generally less than 5 extra tons. I was told by the logistics boys that NASA was a total pain for the bureaucracy, so they minimized requests for cargo lifting—it was usually personal items and pogey bait. Too much paperwork for technical equipment and parts.

Each spacecraft had a lunar lander, and each landing had to be meticulously controlled. Crashing live people on the surface of the Moon would be bad for business. This was the single operation that was 100% controlled by NASA. The Company paid NASA a fee for each transport and was reimbursed (including overheads, direct and indirect costs, and profit) for each fee by the Lunar Authority. The Company made money from each of us from the first day we showed up at the Launch Center in California to three days after we splashed down.

The first day after splashdown, we spent the time getting examined and monitored by the medics aboard the Company recovery ship. Then we had two more days to float back to California. Most of us were in terrible shape, weak and disoriented upon our return. There were recovery and physical therapy services offered at our cost to help us get used to one G again. My first splashdown, I spent two weeks with a recovery service. It cost me $41,000. I tried to do it only one week after my second splashdown, but it was bad. Two weeks was a bare minimum for most people, but it was our choice.

So, splashdown plus three days' examination plus two weeks' recovery, plus it took about 5–6 more weeks for me to finally feel fully normal again after returning dirtside. Two full months gone, but I did not complain—I was making serious dineros on the Moon. At home in New Mexico, I could do pretty much anything I wanted.

I owned a nice house in the Sandia foothills outside Albuquerque. I owned a Rivian R100T pick-up. I illegally disabled the self-drive A.I.—a buddy showed me how. We liked to drag race on the salt flats in Utah. One time I hit 465 KPH. Much higher than this and I would need ceramic tires to avoid blowouts at high speed.

I had nice clothes, some bitching firearms, a superb audio system, and the best HOLO-TV money could buy. I ate like a king, worked out a lot, went hunting and fishing, hung with my friends, and played with the girls. Life was good.

One week prior to the launch date, I had to get a full physical from a Company-authorized doctor. Results had to be presented at the Launch Center 48 hours before launch, where I was subjected to further testing for viruses and bacterial infections, as well as for lice, ticks, rashes, molds, or other parasites. No bugs or germs were permitted on the Moon. One virus outbreak would shut down the entire operation. An infestation of fleas hit the colony in 2059, and it took almost a year to get rid of them all. Even the common cold was forbidden. If I showed up with something, I was quarantined for 5 days (unpaid) and retested. If I failed the follow-up test, I didn't get another launch chance until three months later—three months cut off my 12 months' Moon time. This explains why Moonies are such germophobes when back home. It's not that we are prissy or hypochondriacs, it is because we do not want to lose that all-important Moon money. Most of us didn't save as much as we intended. Most of us partied hard and spent heavily with our big bucks. I dated three different girls back on Earth. Cut off the money stream, and we would become like the rest of the boring Earth drones.

Launch was never easy, but we knew what to expect and we got through it. Landing on the Moon on the fifth day was cake—a soft touchdown. As soon as we disembarked for the holding area (another short quarantine for one day), the re-launch techs swarmed over the lander and gave it loving care. The lander was the most beloved piece of equipment on the Moon. Screw up a lander, and Moonies would likely tear you to pieces and put you through the rock crusher. It was our ticket home. It was going back to The World. It was getting off The Rock. It was life. Lander techs were treated with reverence and respect. We always kept 5 fully fitted-out landers in reserve, in case of issues that the techs could not fix during the short turnaround time allotted to them. Our service bay staff and tools matched anything NASA had back dirtside.

Refueling was the most dangerous part of the operation. LOX and LH2 are damned hard to handle on Earth. It is a worse bitch on the Moon, even with all the robotics. Safety protocols are through the roof. This is why lander techs made more than the other worker bees in the colony, except for the Site Manager, the Chief Engineer, the head of Medical, and the head Psych. To do these jobs in normal Earth gravity without cumbersome pressure suits—even exoskeleton-enhanced pressure suits—was difficult. On the Moon it was life and death every single day.

PART SIX: BREAK-IN

On the 128th day of my third deployment, the tunneling machine broke through to the volcanic bubble. We had the man-camp 98% complete and in the process of stocking for habitation. The advance party was already living there, doing punch-list close-out and Client sign-off (yes, award fee again). We had dug straight down from the surface for 185 meters to establish a semi-protected staging area. From pit bottom, we bored sideways and downwards, from a distance of 1.5 kilometers from the expected location of the bubble, achieving a 10% downward slope. We broke into the bubble at 1.482 kilometers, and the lunar geologists adjusted accordingly. The ground-penetrating radar that located the bubble was not perfect, and they were satisfied with being off by 18 meters. We were hugely lucky to strike a spur, a finger of empty space that made entering the bubble much easier. We did not enter the roof—we had a rock platform for the initial toehold. Without that bubble spur, we would have been forced to build a giant staging platform, all done in zoot suits from suspended scaffolds. Shit.

The cutting head of the boring machine was 8.8 meters in diameter. After sealing the tunnel walls, adding utilities and traction machinery, the tunnel would accommodate three tubes for travel—one down, one up, and one cargo. For a long time, as long as construction took, these would be the means for transporting people, machines, and materials down to the Troll Cave, as we began to call it. The nickname of the mines of Moria was frowned upon by the Company. After the colony was staffed, these same tubes would serve our daily needs. Another shaft was to be dug and bored later, but for now, we were in.

Robotic probes were sent into the huge cavity with cameras and spotlights, seismic sensors, radar, infrared, and drills. They took multiple core samples and brought them back to the scientists for analysis. We needed solid rock to anchor our colony. The core samples were good, the photos and videos were promising, and no anomalies showed up to cause concern. No massive rockfalls were seen. No notable lunar quakes were measured. No poisonous gases detected. They even found some promising ice pockets. Many backs were slapped and hands shaken. The Company was pleased, of course. We never knew where the award fee went—not our concern. We were getting PAID.

With the good news about rock stability, the drilling and anchoring team went to work. Our guys ran coring machines and hammer drills for sinking epoxy anchors into the stone walls, floor, and ceiling. These anchors would support thousands of foundation beams. Then the prefabricated modular units would be installed concurrently with the electrical grid. All water and sewage would be handled internally in modularized treatment plants. Solid waste was burned up to constituent atoms with a giant plasma torch—no need to litter the lunar surface with our trash. Access airlocks, with their attendant dedusting modules and cleansing rooms, would be placed, along with dozens upon dozens of different types of laboratories, utility, maintenance, recreation, eating, farming, and living units. We were building an entire city underground. The heart of the complex would be the atrium farm, with 144 light wells leading up to the surface. These were nearly completed when we started anchoring and foundation operations. The light wells went faster, being only 215 centimeters in diameter. We had six boring machines just for the wells, and they did not break down as often as the main rock hog.

The Company employed a huge engineering team on Earth to design the Lunar Colony underground complex. Seventeen major engineering firms were subcontracted, with over 100 specialty firms and vendors, to produce the fully integrated design and oversee fabrication and packing for launch. A.I. programs were used liberally to minimize mistakes in the coordination of different disciplines and trades and to ensure every module was built perfectly to specification. The modules resembled oversized steel shipping containers that could be bolted together interchangeably. Typical size was 3.5 meters high by 4.5 meters wide by 24.5 meters long. Special rocket stages had to be designed and built to hold eight of these in each launch. They were supplemented with panelized sections in non-standard connection zones. The real challenge was to run fire suppression, power, pressurized air, internet, water, sewer, and other services through multiple module walls, floors, and ceilings without having thousands upon thousands of unnecessary joints between each module. The answer was to install these by hand, the old-fashioned way, with skilled tradesmen. Much construction on Earth was done by robots installing prefab units. On the Moon, there were construction grunts with advanced degrees. The quality control requirements were obscene. Building a nuclear submarine was a walk in the park—child's play compared with what we did on the Moon.

Material costs were roughly $750 billion. Making a prefabricated farming module that could survive lift-off and landing, as well as surface transit and installation down the tunnel, was not cheap. The same could be said for every specialty module—pharmaceutical, microelectronic, nuclear medicine, robotics, zoot suit maintenance—you name it. It was all expensive and all difficult. Shipping costs were another $750 billion. Installation costs (mainly wages) were $150 billion. Engineering was $325 billion. All told, nearly $2 trillion to build this city for 1,000 people, and this did not touch the ongoing operational costs of the current surface colony. It did not touch the costs of maintaining the man-camp for the construction workers. It did not include the cost of personnel transport to and from the

Moon. How would you like to live in a house worth $2 billion? We were getting PAID. Everyone was on board with the program. We were going to ride this nag until it gave out, and then we would all go home.

What could people do that could not be done safer and better (and even cheaper) by A.I.-enabled robots? Not much. The entire premise of the lunar colony was a house of cards. Every one of us knew it, every one of us was getting paid, and every one of us saluted and said, "Yes sir! Yes ma'am!"

The only real benefit for humans on the Moon was for physical rehabilitation, medical research, drug development, retirement living—basically anything that was enhanced by low gravity. The Company knew this. They were milking the program as much as legally possible and creating a new community for retired people, disabled people, sick people. It was like medical tourism that took off in the first half of the 21st century on steroids. Instead of flying to Thailand or India for medical procedures, people could fly to the Moon and live without the pains of old age. They would be light on their feet, mentally alert, challenged by a dynamic new environment, surrounded by smart, talented people.

While low gravity was generally bad for most people, if you were already weak and sick, life was much easier. We were the healthiest people in the world, with fierce control of any invading microbes. We were sanitary as hell. Old people did not need to worry about catching anything on the Moon. They had access to the best nutrition regimen known to science, excellent food, perfect medical care, superb physical rehabilitation, and easy sleep. Sleeping in low G was a dream. For astronauts on the old ISS, it was often difficult to adjust in zero G, but having just 1/6 G was the sweet spot for baby-like dream time.

Another area of development projected much further out into the future was recreation. The Company wanted to develop another volcanic bubble, but this would be strictly for flying. The science fiction author and visionary futurist Robert A. Heinlein came up with the idea in a story over 100 years ago (*The Menace from Earth*). Seal and pressurize a bubble, develop human-powered wing and tail systems that could be worn, and voilà! We can fly! Low lunar gravity made it very possible. The idea was taken very seriously by the advance planners at the Company, and there was vigorous ongoing exploration to find a new bubble. This was considered the holy grail of the lunar colony. If we could build the flight cave, people from all over Earth would come to try their wings.

In addition to the engineering and production of human-powered flight systems, another industry of flight-focused fitness training would spring up, along with flight trainers. Despite the low gravity, it would still require hellacious shoulder muscles to fly on the Moon. I remember reading that the Mongol warriors in Genghis Khan's army shot their bows starting at age five, and by the time they were grown men, they had massive shoulders. Moonies would have a similar look. Traffic police for flyers would be necessary. Wing and tail maintenance shops would be in the mix, and food and beverage courts set up. There would be music, light shows, flight dances, races, and aerobatic competitions. All for a massive fee. The Company was all in on this one. All we had to do was discover another volcanic bubble of adequate size and depth below the surface.

PART SEVEN: CONSTRUCTION

I hardly ever got to see Sharia now that I was permanently deployed to the man-camp. This sucked big-time, but I was getting OT every single week, so this helped offset my disappointment a little bit. Still, I missed her a lot. I had long fantasized about meeting her back dirtside and getting married and having a couple of kids. She avoided the subject. Maybe she had a main squeeze back in Iran. No knowing—she never said.

I was assigned supervision of anchor and beam installation. This needed to be done before the sealant guys went to town. No need to damage newly installed sealant coating. They would seal around every anchor, in addition to sealing the overall chamber. Six coats of flexible aramid-polymer, tough as Kevlar but durable in the temperature extremes of the Moon, would yield a sealant thickness of 9.5 millimeters, + or − 1 mm. All to be inspected by QC technicians, all to be supervised by engineers, all to be tested for airtightness. Everyone had his job, and everyone was getting PAID.

But first we had to get the anchors and beams in. The interior surface area of the Bat Cave was roughly 1.54 million square meters for purposes of anchorage. The sealant guys had to account for all the nooks and crannies and cracks, so they were looking at 2.65 million square meters of actual surface area. We sank anchors every 100 square meters, so this meant 15,400 anchors. We drilled in anywhere from 1.6 meters to 2.2 meters deep—all determined by the lunar geologists. They gave us a 3-D drill map (checked by QC and logged, of course) every shift. Each hole had to be angled correctly into the rough-surfaced rock for the anchor steel to stand out to the right location for beam attachment.

We ran 12-hour shifts, 6 days a week. We did not have enough technicians to do two shifts. We were freaking wiped-out exhausted every single day. Our hands and wrists were cramped and clawed. Our backs and arms and legs ached something fierce. If you think work is easy in low G, try doing it inside a zoot suit. Try avoiding punctures and burns and chemical attacks. Every single day coming back in, we went through the same de-dusting routine. Each of us had two suits—one for work and one being cleaned and checked while we worked, to be swapped out the next day.

A zoot suit costs about $97,500,000 to manufacture, plus shipping costs, plus maintenance kits, ancillary systems, plus compressed air and water and hell rat consumption. Real replacement cost was closer to $110,000,000, especially since the suit manufacturer (on-site suit techs were third-tier subs) contracted by the Company was always doing upgrades. No problem—it was cost-plus. Anchors that passed final inspection got a small award fee. Got to get that award fee!

We did not get a break from the mandatory 2 hours PT, and we were required to show up for chow twice a day (lunch was eaten inside the suit on-site. Hell rats). We had to do a written log at the end of every shift. This left zero down time—all of us just zonked at the end of the day. All socializing was done during daily chit-chat and razzing while working. Limited alcohol and marijuana were permitted at the man-camp, but none of us cared. Too tired. Stimulants were forbidden by policy, and I am not saying there were no stims used during construction. I avoided them because they gave you a false sense of strength and vitality. They were great for emergency situations, like a medevac, or if you ever got lost on the surface, but I did not like the crash that always followed. We ate like horses, slept like logs, and did our workouts. We were just machines that made MONEY 12 hours a day.

My crew of anchor installers never got bigger than 18 guys. None was a slacker or complainer. Any asshole who was hard to work with got shit-canned, usually by group consensus. I was fair and straight with my guys, and they performed. If someone screwed up, I made him explain his error and tell me how he was gonna fix it. Then I lightly slapped his helmet, called him a jackass, grinned at him, and told him he was beautiful, and sent him back to work. I never humiliated any of the men, and they never hid fuckups from me.

Leadership is not hard if your team sees you are human, work just as hard as they do, and keep things light. I always kept a clear strategy and schedule out in front of them. We had a job to do to get paid the crazy stupid money we were getting, and we did it.

A 1.9-meter hole typically took four hours to drill. It was a two-step process. First, we used the core drilling machine cutting a cylindrical slot, 95 mm in diameter, in the rock. That core slot had to be lined up no-shit-honest-to-God perfect. Then we augered it out with a hammer-drill. Why this tedious way? Because the structural engineering wienies determined that to simply hammer-drill everything would introduce micro-fractures in the rock and weaken the connection, making it more prone to failure. Their word was gospel, and we did the two-step.

Multiply 4 hours 15,400 times and you got 61,600 hours of just coring and drilling. Divide this by 18 men and it was 3,422 hours per man on average. Actual work time was closer to 9 hours when you subtract suit-up and dust-down time, as well as scheduled breaks. This meant it was going to take us roughly 380 workdays (64 work weeks), just for anchor holes. We blew through thousands of coring cylinders and hammer drill bits—all carbide tipped, all shipped from Earth at $250 per kilogram, on top of actual purchased cost. The cost just to manufacture and ship the anchor bars was roughly $600 million, not counting the labor of transporting to site and into the active construction zone, plus our installation cost.

Since I had dirtside rotations to coordinate, sick-bay visits, suit leaks, equipment malfunctions, and sheer fatigue to contend with, the real time was closer to 70 weeks. There was not much float in the schedule—20 days—and we were on the critical path. Delay the anchorage and we delay the entire construction project. Not good. Then the Company must try to explain delays in EVMS jargon, including a recovery plan and lessons learned. Then we had to come up with some kind of way to actually recover the schedule (not even vaguely possible). In a pinch, the Company could go to the client, hat in hand, and ask for an extension. This was deeply frowned upon. I was sure that I would suffer eternal damnation if I caused this humiliation. Technically, as a cost-plus operation, any schedule delay would be paid by the client, but they could demand a change in senior management, and senior management did not want this. Can't fund the 80-meter yacht operations in the Mediterranean staffed with hookers from China if they were not on the gravy train.

The actual anchors were Fe-Cr-Ni-C grade, cryogenically hardened, martensitic stainless-steel solid bars, 83 mm in diameter, protruding 1.4 to 2.7 meters from the rock face. Before placement we reamed out the dust in the hole with a wire brush, followed by a blast of nitrogen gas. The protruding end of the anchor was precisely positioned, to within 2 mm in any direction, so this was the touchiest part of the process. Each anchor was checked and rechecked by QC prior to insertion of the cementitious epoxy material, which required 15 minutes for initial set (after the hole was pre-heated), during which time we double-checked end placement again. If we were off, we had to extract and clean the hole and start over—a very ugly and tedious procedure, overseen by prissy QC technicians. The Company frowned on errors. My team was shit hot. We knew what fuckups meant, and we were ruthless with each other for perfection. I made sure the coring machines recorded every single borehole angle and inclination, so we could re-drill precisely if we had to.

To set 15,400 anchors we needed another 2 hours per anchor—another 35 weeks of schedule time, based on our 18-man crew. This was followed by the beam welding process—15,400 titanium beams with stainless weld gussets attached to the anchor studs with 100% inspected welds. Beams were installed on every wall and roof (for hanging rods), as well as the floor. The entire city would be integrated structurally. More award fees, of course. To weld one wide-flanged beam on both ends was two hours, plus inspection time, plus set-up and moving time. A beam weighed 910 kilograms (152 kg in Moon weight). Safety protocol required four men to move a beam in place. My team cheated and did it with two, with no accidents. We learned how to use our eight-legged, robotic cherry pickers to the best efficiency. On-site safety technicians were always in short supply, so we got away with it.

On and on and on and on it went. Month after month of 12-hour days, six days a week. Every 60 days we got a short, 4-day R&R back at the main colony. I looked up my black-haired hottie and we lit up the sheets. I was never sure if she had another lay on the side, but she always showed up with a big smile when I called her for bootie time. "I missed you, Jeremy!" she would say, "why do you have to be gone so much?" God, I couldn't figure her out! She made me crazy. Then I was back out in the Troll Cave, setting anchors and welding beams.

We needed more crews. I screamed and pleaded and threatened. Management was very sympathetic. They had job postings out all over the world. They offered major signing bonuses. But we needed very intense and specific skills. Non-hackers, bozos, and fake techs would not do the job we needed to be done. They were inundated with thousands of applications. Out of 1,000 of these, we might get 2 truly qualified people. Even then, they had to pass the psych and physical exams, go through training, and basically sign away their lives. Newbies trickled in at a snail's pace.

At the same time, there was a steady drain of old, used-up Moonies who had enough and needed to get out before they burned out completely. Our medical group had a big psychiatric section. Moonies were generally a neurotic bunch, and this high-stress work took its toll.

I was close to the edge myself. Sharia was my steam release valve. I had thought to stay my third year and get out, but the Company waved a huge re-signing bonus under my nose, with additional home leave time, and I caved. I signed for two more years of back-breaking, soul-crushing labor. But hey, I was getting PAID.

PART EIGHT: COPS

The Lunar Colony boasted an average IQ of 159—no one on-site with an IQ lower than 137. Out of 1,003 people, 63% had PhDs. Of these, 80 had TWO PhDs. Of these, 28 had THREE PhDs. Only one person on the Moon had anything less than a master's, and he had a double bachelor's in math and physics (both earned at age 17), plus he was an expert in polymeric physics just from his own hobby research. He was on the cave-sealing membrane team as a field operator. Sharia held a PhD in horticulture. She never lorded over my lowly master's.

Nevertheless, you would think with all that brainpower that Moonies would be better behaved, more sensible, more able to resolve personal conflicts. You would be wrong. We had our share of sociopaths (more than our share, actually), narcissists, prissy prima donnas, whiny irresponsible adults, backstabbers, liars, and arrogant, entitled assholes. The fact of confinement in close quarters did not make human relations a happy experience on the Moon. Professional disputes easily degenerated into screaming and name-calling. There were fistfights, property damage, long-simmering resentments, backstabbing, sabotage—you name it. We were quite the difficult crew to manage.

You would think that people who were paid such ungodly money would have the sense to protect their jobs, to behave and get along. No. In fact, just the opposite. Moonies generally felt their shit did not stink. They thought of themselves as indispensable. So, we did not have a happy colony all the time.

The Company was forced to hire private security to police the colony. They did not boast the same IQs as the operations staff, but the average private dick was still pretty sharp. No one in the security force had an IQ lower than 115—the average was about 130. No firearms were carried on the Moon (although it was rumored that there was an armory just in case an insurrection broke out). The cops were armed with batons, tasers, tangle-web, handcuffs, and sleepy gas. They were all very well trained in martial arts, methods of restraining suspects, conflict resolution, and negotiation. They were mostly well-behaved, but from time to time there were issues.

We had a lock-up area for badly behaved Moonies to go for time-out. Judicial proceedings were run by lawyers and judges hired by the same company that provided the cops, so they worked hand in glove. Time-out was authorized for public intoxication, illegal drugs, theft, assault, deliberate damage, and a handful of other infractions. These were usually accompanied by a stiff fine—anywhere from $10,000 to $75,000. When the first team of police showed up 19 years back, it took some getting used to, but Moonies finally accepted. Everyone was required to sign a compliance clause in their contracts, and we had to read and resign yearly. Punishment ranged from lock-up for 1–3 days (with reduced pay plus fine), lock-up for 4–7 days (with no pay plus fine), up to ejection from the colony. Even this was not permanent. If you returned dirtside and kept your nose clean, went to re-education classes, passed the psych eval, and signed a good-boy sheet, you were permitted to return to the colony. The Company was paid for every warm body on the Moon—it was in their best interests to recycle offenders, assuming they could not find qualified replacements. It was a "three strikes and you're out" policy. This contributed to the fearlessness of so many to break rules—they knew the penalties were relatively minor.

The security team monitored all the video and audio feeds from all over—especially watching video of teams out on the surface. You never knew when an event would happen. They were trained to suit up quickly and head outside in case some muscle was ever needed (they were also trained in emergency rescue and first aid). Speaking of muscle, none of these guys was smaller than 1.90 meters and 100 kilos. They had their own gym for strength and self-defense training.

Tommy Washington was a friend of mine in the police force. He was a huge, bright, Black, veteran Marine from the West Texas oilfields, born in Trinidad, with an IQ of 145. I am pretty big—the same size as the smaller cops—but he was 10 centimeters taller and 35 kilos heavier—all muscle. I did a lot of my workouts with

Tommy in their gym, and he pushed me near to breaking. He worked for two years as a physical fitness instructor in the Marine Corps before becoming a scout-sniper. We had specially designed resistance training equipment that multiplied the actual weight we were lifting by 6. On Earth in college, I had bench-pressed 140 kilograms. Tommy pushed me up to 180. I called him the Jolly Green Giant, and he would just grin and slap my back with a hand the size and weight of a Thanksgiving turkey and say, "I like you, Jeremy! Time to lift again, only a lot harder! You are not giving me enough! You gotta give me EVERYTHING!" He shouted at me in his West Texas, Trinidad, basso profundo voice: "Lift, Jeremy! Goddamn you LIFT!" He was bellowing in my face while, I swear, blood was squirting from my eyeballs. I was destroyed—obliterated—after every workout with Tommy. He offered to help get me on the police force—I was an expert marksman and had boxed in college. It would get me out of the grueling outside work, but I declined. I am too much of a gearhead to step away from engineering. Plus, my pay was much better.

Despite all the struggles of policing a bunch of privileged, backstabbing, brilliant prima donnas, the cops kept a cheerful and professional demeanor. Their contracts (and Company lawyers) protected them, and they were getting PAID. All on cost-plus. No award fee, though. Keeping people OUT of lock-up was considered the minimum requirement by the Lunar

Authority. Every single case of misdemeanor and crime was investigated ad infinitum.

As long as the peace was maintained and no significant damage or injury occurred, the Company was happy. They were VERY sensitive to presenting a happy face to the residents of Earth. They strove mightily to portray the Moon as a wonderful place for rehabs and retirees, a place that was safe, adventurous, healthful, and grand. Having stories of Moonies being beaten by cops would not go over well in dirtside media.

There had been two incidents of brutally serious ass-stomping (permanent, crippling injuries) by the police in their 19-year history on the Moon, and two unlawful deaths. Seventeen illegal chokings and forty-eight other excessive force violations. They were protected by Company lawyers and strongly worded contracts. If they misbehaved, their wrists were slapped. The Company paid heavy settlements to the families, made notes in personnel files, required additional training, and put the cops back to work. They faced fines, re-training classes, and temporary deportation back to Earth. A cop could even be put in lock-up, but it never happened. Nevertheless, most of the cops were decent guys (no females on our force).

One thing that helped to keep them happy was the sex trade. Both male and female prostitutes were brought to the colony, disguised as tourists, and they set up house in the police quarters area. They kept the boys happy, as well as a few Moonies who wanted to pay serious cash for some sexual fun. No one was allowed more than 30 minutes, and this cost $2,000 (credited on Company terminals as "Recreation—General"). The visitors worked on average about 6–8 hours a day. They got to keep all the credit, as long as the security force got freebies. This was the rent payment by the hookers. They typically stayed for about 90 days and went home with half a million dollars or better. These were all A-team hookers, both male and female—stunningly beautiful, physically fit, free of STDs, and sexually wild. They knew their trade and knew their clients, and they provided superb service. When the EVMS auditors visited, they lay low and kept quiet—no stupid ones in this crew.

PART NINE: CITY

Container units started showing up as soon as the beam welding was far enough ahead of the module installation crews to not be overrun. For them it was a point of pride to run up the ass of my beam team and then complain bitterly about our delays. I was ruthless with my guys about quality—any fuckups caused serious setbacks, and we had to listen not only to the ragging from the module guys but also sit in a "fact-finding" session with management. These were documented, recorded, videoed, and gruelingly long. The suckiness of these sessions cannot be overstated. We already knew exactly why we made a mistake. We already knew what to do to prevent similar ones in the future. It was punishment and blame-setting, even though human resources explained very carefully that it was not. You knew they were looking for victims and culprits. Sit through one fact-finding and you will swear you will kill someone before you sit through another one. I would rather poke myself in the eye with a sharp stick. You could cut the political correctness in these sessions with a knife. As team leader, I had to sit through every one of them when my guys were involved.

The module guys were tickled pink. We were kept separated during off-hours because of the potential for fights. I will never take shit against my crew. We stand together, we screw up together, we make it right

47

together. Simple. I discovered one time that my guys had whipped the asses of three module people who had conspired to jump me and beat me. I never knew about it until I got challenged by their team leader, who complained about my people "bullying" his. I bought booze and stim tabs for my team after this.

I had a few quiet words with some of the QC engineers, and they went back and discovered dozens and dozens of incompletely bolted module connections. The entire module team went through fact-finding, follow-up training, and added oversight after this. Their team leader was fired. Shortcuts could cost the Company award fees, and this was strenuously reinforced to the module crew leadership and engineers, ad infinitum, ad nauseam. They had a very long fact-finding session. You do NOT fuck the Company. Pressure on my beam team died way down.

Despite the early game-playing, the bubble shell grew and developed like a giant LEGO-Land city, eventually reaching 2,776 modules in 32 levels from bottom to top. As modules were certified, the interior fit-out teams came in for utility runs and equipment setting. Some equipment came to us already installed, but some had to be field-fit after preliminary utility work was done. Our chief electrical manager had a PhD in power systems, as well as being a qualified master electrician in 22 U.S. states. Our chief mechanical superintendent held a PhD in mechanical engineering—HVAC and thermal control systems—as well as being a qualified pipe and steam fitter—union member for 32 years. No bozos on the construction teams—every one of us was tough, smart, workaholic, and gifted at problem-solving. The module crew eventually played nice, and fights became a thing of the past.

The underground city became the shining showcase of the Company. Important visitors from around the world came for visits. Champagne was enjoyed liberally, gourmet food was eaten (Maine lobster on the Moon!), outside trips were provided. Surreptitious visits to the police barracks for playtime were quietly arranged. The supporters of our flagship project were impressed, vowing undying support for our work with their home governments. Our visitors received complimentary tickets to the World Cup, the Super Bowl, and the Olympics. They got trips on the yachts, served by beautiful staff. How do you spend $2 trillion? You do it with STYLE, baby! Keep those launches going! Keep delivering goods and materials to the Moon! Keep building, boys! We love you for it!

I continued for most of my fourth year on the Rock setting anchors and welding beams. I took my 60-day R&Rs and got hooked up with Sharia. I was allowed a shorter stay (11 months) by my new contract, and I took my home leave on schedule. I did a one-week handover to my replacement, a super-sharp guy named Mofufu. The crew loved him. He was a tiny guy from Ghana, all of 1.62 meters tall, maybe 50 kilos, and his speech was faster than lightning. At 182, his IQ was through the roof, even for the Lunar Colony. He was all in for getting the job done, and the crew embraced him and his crazy ways. "Don't worry about us, Jeremy," they told me, "We'll watch his back. He is too fun to allow anything bad to happen." I felt better. I packed my trash and got onto the return launch for Earth.

PART TEN: HOME

After I went through recovery and rested and recuperated for a couple of months, I ran into a wall. None of my friends could relate to anything I had to say. They loved my prosperity, and I had all sorts of cool stuff, but they were boring to me. I found myself getting irritated with them easily. I stopped calling, and they stopped coming over. They could see my sullen mood. Two or three had some serious brain power, but even they were all tied up with Earth- and U.S.A.-related issues. They simply did not understand what it meant to be a Moonie. They did not WANT to understand.

I fell into depression. I was psychologically exhausted. My body did not like 1G. I wasn't sleeping well. I snapped at strangers, then apologized, and then felt like shit. What the hell was wrong with me? I started to go to bars. I got into a bad fight with two guys—they nearly destroyed me; I was hurt badly. Note to self: do NOT get into fights with rednecks who have buddies behind you. I needed facial reconstructive surgery to fix my nose, facial bones, and teeth—five operations. The cracked ribs from their boot kicks took forever to heal. Second note to self: do NOT get drunk when you are alone. Nobody will help your dumb ass, and you might get robbed. Or killed. Albuquerque is a tough town.

I got into a nasty argument with my good friend, Tyler. He was a PhD graduate at M.I.T., working in post-doc research. I met him at Western Michigan. He gave me his unvarnished view: "Jeremy, I don't know why you think you're special. You have a job that pays stupid money. You seem to think you are different from everybody else, and you don't give a shit about what happens here on Earth. Well, guess what, son? Who do you think PAYS for all your space fun? And do you actually care about anything here?" He was right. I could not care less about politics or social problems or pollution. We didn't have any of these issues on the Moon. He knew it, and it pissed him off. "Why do you even come back here, if you don't give a shit about us?" I suggested he apply for a job on the Moon, and he cut me off. "FUCK the Moon!" I was shocked. I thought he was envious of my money and position, but there was much more to it than that. He truly hated what we were.

Tyler at least said something useful. "Do you even know what you want to be when you grow up? You have been playing astronaut for four years, and you don't even know where you're going! Besides that, you always have this attitude about being better than everyone else!" His words stung. They were too close to the truth. I didn't like it a bit, but I had nothing to say. He was right.

What did it mean to be a Moonie? Hell if I knew, but I was sure that life on Earth was not as exhilarating, challenging, or deeply social as the Lunar Colony. I had over $2.8 million in the bank at age 30. My house, truck, and personal goods were all paid for. I even bought 225 acres in Colorado for fishing and hunting. I did not enjoy fishing and hunting very much anymore. I went out to the gun range to shoot, and it wasn't as fun as it used to be. I thought about Sharia all the time. Every time I thought about her, no matter how intellectual or romantic my thoughts were, I always ended up jacking off. There were hot women in Albuquerque, hot women who wanted to be with me. To me, they were boring and shallow. I love a hot woman as much as the next guy, but she needs to have a soul and character and a brain (like Sharia). I traveled a lot—Europe, South America, New Zealand. Much of it was fun, there were some awesome sights, but I missed Sharia, and I missed my crazy-ass Moonie job and work crew. I entered into deep depression. I had no idea what I wanted.

I looked into getting a PhD, and several excellent schools were ready to take me. I could have gone to the Sorbonne, to Kyoto, to Oxford, to Moscow, to Stanford, to M.I.T. I had the test scores and grades. What to study? I already knew more about mechanical engineering than most of the PhD professors. I knew how metals in severe cold reacted to stress and heat, coefficients of friction, modulus of elasticity—the works. I was possibly the best welder in the Solar System. I knew how lubricants could best be utilized in a vacuum. I knew how to calculate pressures and mechanical advantage and throughput. I had fully memorized the maintenance manuals on mining equipment worth hundreds of millions of dollars. I was steeped in Lunar engineering up to my ears. On the Moon I worked with literally the best minds in the Solar System. Why work hard learning things I already understood expertly, just to get a piece of paper that proved I was smart?

I thought about the design of the Troll Cave, and how I would improve on its development. I thought about the flight cave, and how to make it work for the maximum number of people. On a whim, I decided to call the Company and see if I could get through to their engineering department. I told them who I was and was told someone would get back to me. Fat chance, I thought, but two days later the deputy head of recreational engineering gave me a call. We talked for over two hours on the phone as I shared a few ideas. Two days later I flew to the engineering campus in Geneva. They took me very seriously. I spent three days talking with different department heads, and when I was done, the head of recruiting asked to see me.

"Jeremy, we are extremely impressed with your ideas and your energy. We want to use your brains and talent more effectively in the Lunar Program." "Glad to hear it," I replied, "what's on your mind?" I felt flattered—I saw myself as just another field grunt. "We need a head for liaison engineering, to work at the colony and coordinate design development and field execution." "I would be based at the main colony, and not out at the man camp?" I asked. SHARIA. Bells were ringing in my head. I am sure that steam was coming out of my ears. My dick started to get hard as I sat there in my nice suit. "Yes, although there would be trips out to the construction site a couple of times a month for a few days each. We also want to put you through some complex computer-interface training, to get you on board with the A.I. systems. That will be about seven months or so. It is incredibly intense—you will be totally immersed in an A.I. computer program, eight hours a day. It would need to happen during your current home leave if you don't mind. We will pay you at your base rate while training, and when you complete and re-deploy, your new salary will be $1.45 million. You will be the new director of systems coordination for the human-powered flight program. This is the third-ranking engineering position in the entire program." "It isn't a problem that I don't have a PhD?" "After you complete the A.I. program, you will be awarded a PhD by Harvard. It is an extremely intense course. Our program is the best on Earth. They asked us for the privilege of sponsoring the training—we did not ask them. Your doctoral thesis will be actual execution of the program at the Colony. Yes, you will need to thoroughly document all your work and present it to a board. It will be a legitimate, earned PhD. You will be the first doctor of lunar engineering." I felt dizzy. I am sure my eyes were glazed.

"One more thing," she added, "at your level, there are specific Company benefits that are not available to all the staff. You are eligible for permanent residency on the Moon, all paid, with paid retirement pension, medical, the whole package, if you so choose. The retirement includes annual Earth trips, if you wish, but with not so many restrictions. No obligation on your part—it is just a senior-management benefit we offer." "What happens if I get married? Would my wife be allowed to stay with me, with all coverage?" "Yes, no question." "Where do I sign?" "There's no rush," she replied, "if you want to think about it a bit." "Perhaps you did not understand me... WHERE DO I SIGN?" She smiled, "We will have the documents prepared tomorrow morning for electronic signature. Enjoy your evening here in Geneva."

That evening in the hotel, I placed a call to Sharia. Amazingly, she answered on the first ring. She sounded genuinely pleased to hear my voice. "Hi hot baby!" The usual pause as the signal ran 770,000 kilometers round trip. "Hi super-stud!" (pause) "Well, now that we got the formalities out of the way, I want to tell you some interesting news. But first, I want you to tell me about your farming plans on the Moon. ALL your farming plans." (pause) "Oh? That's interesting. I thought you were more of a gearhead, and this biological stuff (with certain exceptions) was of no interest." (pause) "Smart ass! Tell me anyway. I have a very specific reason for asking."

Sharia is smart—crazy smart. I heard she had the second- or third-highest IQ on the Moon. She loved her work, and she had developed amazing strains of vegetables and herbs that thrived in low G. She managed pollination with honeybees in low G. She worked out the problems of bovine digestion and sheep gestation, making raising animals feasible on the Moon. She did work in gene editing, epigenetic disease resistance, and even cooking techniques in low G. Her curiosity was boundless. For a long time, I thought she was bored with me and only wanted me for sex. It turned out she was afraid of boring ME and bowed out gracefully when we finished our romping. I was wrong. She thought I was really smart (this from a flaming genius!?) and she knew nothing about mechanical engineering. She was impressed with how hard I worked long hours in the heavy zoot suit without complaining. She was intimidated. Huh???

I told her how fascinated I was by her work, and I meant it. Food production was incredible. It guaranteed the future of the Lunar Colony. I always loved walking through the farming areas of the colony. I loved the smells and the colors and the sounds. It reminded me of my great-grandfather's ranch near Artesia in New Mexico. He was a retired U.S. Senator who taught me how to shoot when I was six. His pecan grove was his pride and joy. "Do you think you could grow pecans?" I asked. "I would have to check the water demand, but I don't see why not." It was incredibly complex and difficult, and I told her how impressed I was with her brainpower and work ethic. She needed to continue her work and have every chance to succeed, and make the colony succeed. I could fairly feel her glowing over the phone link.

Then she switched on the video feed. She was stark naked. To say Sharia was gorgeous naked was like saying the Pacific Ocean is vast. Her nakedness exploded my brain—it always did. She stood up and did a little low-G dance for me, stroking her body all over while she danced. "I sure wish you would hurry and come back to the Moon, Jeremy!" She was truly an evil woman. I loved her!

Then I told her about the Company's plan for me. She shrieked with happiness. "I thought you had decided not to come back to the Moon! I was SO worried!" She jumped up and down in slow-motion low G, her big boobs floating up and down. I was going insane.

"So, what do you think about having children? Have you ever thought about it?" I just blurted it out—and immediately regretted it. Did I screw up all of a sudden? (pause)

She shrieked again. Jumped up and down again, boobs floating again. "I take that as a positive response?" (pause) "You are BAD!" she replied. (pause) "Yes, I am bad, and I am crazy in love with YOU!" (pause) "Yes, yes, YES, you stupid man! But, what about the Company? If I get pregnant, I will be in trouble." (pause) "Maybe I can arrange a compromise," I answered. There are perks with being in senior management.

The next day I discussed my hope with the HR director, Dr. Lee. She did not bat an eyelash. "I am sure the Company can give serious consideration to your request, especially since you are one of our top scientists already deployed." (It felt weird to be called a top scientist. I thought I was a gearhead.) "There would need to be some policy discussions, some procedures for how to handle a birth—if you chose to have the child on the Moon. Childcare is non-existent now. We would need a pediatrician. There are even some political considerations regarding citizenship. To be honest, we have already been discussing this possibility. The wave of the future is to make the Moon a permanent habitation for society, and not just for the old. A growing society needs children, yes?"

I smiled. The rules are made for the little people in big organizations. The higher-ups can bend the rules to suit themselves whenever they want. This is an immutable rule of life. So? I decided to let them bend the rules in my favor. Sharia loves high-tech farming. I love engineering. We love each other. It was time to move the Moon forward into a new world of family life.

FLIGHT CAVE
PART ONE: NEW BUBBLE

We had been working on fitting out the new Troll Cave for two years, when the new flight bubble was discovered. It was almost under our noses- only 220 meters deeper than the troll cave, and 2.5 kilometers away. It was less than half the size of the habitation bubble- 600 meters long, 580 meters wide, 365 meters deep. We had our flight venue. The Company senior execs were giddy. Champaign glasses clinked. Their business plan was very well developed, with resources planned and committed.   We began tunneling immediately. No time to lose.

There was not nearly as much preparatory work needed to get the flight bubble up and operational. The biggest cost element was the gigantic HVAC system. We had to condition, circulate, filter, humidify, and heat over 67 million cubic meters of air at 1 bar pressure. The habitation HVAC systems in the living and working cave were divided into 237 discrete systems (with associated dehumidifiers and CO_2 scrubbers) for the various modules and work areas. The flight room (now christened the Bat Cave) would have three power sources—the main, the rotational back-up, and emergency. The ambient temperature this far below the lunar surface was stunningly cold—minus 230 °C, about 43 degrees above absolute zero. While the living modules were all insulated heavily, the entire flight cave would need to be coated internally with 50 centimeters of spray foam, on top of the rock sealant. We had the technology to apply foam that could withstand huge temperature differentials without cracking, but it had to be applied five centimeters at a time. The interior surface area of the flight cave was over 800,000 square meters. This meant we applied 400,000 cubic meters of foam. Over 40,000 cubic meters of foam had to be applied ten times. Wearing pressure suits. In near-absolute-zero cold. Every piece of equipment had to be man-portable. Following strict safety protocols. It was a daunting prospect.

Thankfully, we retained the same electrical and mechanical superintendents that worked the Troll Cave. Back when I had the anchor stud crew, they called me "wonder boy the welder." Now, I was "the fuckin' engineer." No problem—they promoted me. I remember discussing field coordination conflicts with one or the other. A few times I offered solutions that were efficient and effective. The superintendent would grunt, grudgingly admitting to himself (but not to me) that maybe I wasn't such a dolt after all.

Thank goodness for Mofufu! Yes, we still had my beam team replacement superintendent with us. He was a pistol. He was a high velocity bullet with a tungsten carbide tip. He lived for the challenge. While I was away on Earth, he got the beam crew to increase production by 7% over my best efforts, and all without any complaints from the guys. They loved him. He was also loved by a tiny little medical doctor from Wuhan named Fang Zhe Chen. She was 1.47 meters tall and weighed all of 40 kilos back on Earth. They fell for each other like an avalanche.

Despite the classic Chinese racism against Africans, her family thought Mofufu was the best thing since sliced bread. They fawned over him. She was terribly nervous introducing him to her traditional-minded parents when they were both on dirtside leave, but in the first 60 seconds he had them eating out of his hand. He showed spotless deference and respect yet was bursting with smiles and laughter. He was irresistible. His smile dazzled with humor and his eyes flashed with joy. His charm was bigger than Mt. Everest. If anything, he became even more of a fireball with his hot little Fang to inspire him. So, Mofufu set out to plan and execute the mountainous task of insulating the cave.

The Company encouraged such liaisons and relationships openly. For many years they remained coolly neutral to romantic relationships and did not permit married couples to work in the same areas together. With the breakthrough allowed for Sharia and me, it was as if suddenly the Company smiled on marriage like a Baptist preacher. A wedding chapel was installed. Marriage counselors rotated through on a temporary basis. The general psychological well-being of the entire colony improved measurably. People like to live together in committed relationships. It was almost as if the past 200,000 years of human evolution were vindicated. Who knew?

Planning for baby and toddler nurseries was begun. Sharia and I had our first baby, a wild little boy named Tycho—we nicknamed him the Lunatic. Tycho was born on Earth—she had her first four months of pregnancy on the Moon, but neither of us was brave enough to do a full gestation and birth on the Moon. We also wanted to ensure his citizenship. After the overthrow of the ayatollahs, the United States and Iran had finally settled their differences, back at the Treaty of Ankara in 2045, and dual citizenship was permitted.

Sharia stayed on Earth with the Lunatic for one entire year after his birth. It was awful being separated so long, but he needed to develop in full Earth G before going to the Moon. He would be the first baby in space, and the Company made a big PR deal over it. He was going to be a guinea pig, but we did not wish to push the envelope too far. His being a guinea pig also inspired another nickname for him: Baby Pig. This was due to his talent for smearing and mushing food into his hair, his ears, his belly button, his butt-cheek crack, and his genitals. He was totally disgusting, and we became adept at quick clean-ups. I was grateful to almighty God that we did not live in zero G. Baby diarrhea is daunting enough on Earth. On the Moon, it took us to the limit of human endurance.

My job was to coordinate the mechanical and electrical engineers charged with creating and testing our HVAC systems, along with tying them to a redundant power grid. Power was supplied by an entirely new solar farm. This alone took a year and a half to assemble and install, after a year of fabrication and four months of launches from Earth, with 250 workers and 50 robots. It included massive capacitor banks and battery storage. We needed 200 megawatts to heat and circulate, as well as to power the HEPA filters for the air, plus all ancillary systems such as tunnel transportation, light, and service power. Our 32 air-handling units weighed 16 tons each, Earth mass. We had 165 giant recirculation fans, distributed in 49 locations. We were not designing simply for breathing—we were designing for efficient flight. We needed manageable air currents that we could map for flyers. Our Harvard A.I. design systems were the best ever developed. We modeled birds. We modeled bats. We modeled dragonflies. We modeled humans. We modeled windstorms. We put actual humans into wind tunnels, first on Earth, and then we built a test wind tunnel on the Moon to test mock-up flight suits in lunar G. Then we incorporated our findings into cave airflow design.

How to pressurize this volume with air, heated air? The living modules and work areas had multiple, redundant air-pressure systems—the entire colony was not dependent on one or two systems. Multiple automated airlocks in corridors segregated areas in case of explosive decompression or fire. But 67 million cubic meters at one atmosphere of pressure? This is over 82 thousand tons of air that must be produced or shipped. If we depended on electrolysis of water for oxygen, then at 20.9% of overall mass, we would need over 17 thousand tons. The amount of pure ice needed to produce this much oxygen was over 19.3 thousand tons. By 2087, the ice miners were producing enough for the original colony, the man-camp, and enough for construction activities in the Troll Cave—about 50 tons per week. We could expand electrolysis production, but there was no way we could ramp up mining to come close to meeting the need for oxygen.

Did I mention humidity? For 50% relative humidity at 20 °C, we need 615 tons of water in the air. We needed to manage condensation, rust, bacteria, and mold in the flight cave, along with 100 other issues. Would it rain in there? We did not know, so we ran the problem through the design program. The A.I. said no—not enough thermal or moisture differential in colliding air masses. We would not even have clouds or fog, which was a relief.

What about a trip to Saturn? We could send a spacecraft to capture a huge chunk of ice from the rings (à la *Raiders from the Rings*, by Andre Norton) and ferry it back to the Moon. It was feasible, and with the recently perfected atomic electric propulsion system, we could make fairly good time, but it would still take five years. The program cost would exceed $250 billion just for the Saturn project.

Carve up Antarctica and launch ice to the Moon? Even if it could be approved politically (nearly impossible with global warming in full swing), the heavy-lift costs alone would exceed $4 billion, not to mention setting up a huge ice-mining operation in the harshest climate on Earth and shipping the ice in insulated containers to a spaceport. Total cost would exceed $25 billion. We would also need to increase our electrolysis operations tenfold—another $31 billion. Somehow, we also needed to produce nitrogen. Fractional distillation of liquefied air on Earth was the answer—nitrogen was incredibly abundant. Distill it and freeze it and ship it to the Moon for $36 billion. Stealing oxygen from Earth's atmosphere was a bridge too far, but nitrogen harvesting was no problem. Ice mining and launching was the decided method. The colony got to keep the leftover H_2 that came out of the electrolysis—all negotiated by Company contract lawyers.

The Company did not blink at $92 billion. This was a few months of operating costs. They had deep pockets, and they could buy many politicians and bureaucrats, enough to approve the Antarctic mining project. So, they did. The Company wanted that flight cave, and what the Company wanted, the Company got.

PART TWO: WINGS

The idea of flying on the Moon took off like a rocket back on Earth. It filled the popular consciousness to overflowing. Human-powered flight! The exhilaration of being a bird! Freedom! Adventure! Athletic competition! It was all there. Wing and tail design competitions were started, and thousands of teams participated. The cash prizes were enormous—$100 million for first place, with $25 million and $10 million for second and third. The following-on manufacturing contracts would be lucrative as well.

The Company sponsored presentations on HOLO-TV by renowned ornithologists and aeronautical engineers, and physicists discussing air flow and pressure. They hired physical fitness experts to develop training routines to prepare human shoulders and backs for flight in low G. They sold reservations for $100 million each—twice the cost of a standard Moon vacation package. Over 2,000 were bought within the first three months. It seemed that every billionaire on the planet was ready to fly. Anyone worried about financing the ice launches was quickly pacified with this result.

Resources were scaled back from the underground colony and diverted to the flight cave. We had enough modules installed for most of the regular colony staff to relocate. Sharia and Tycho were on the way to me again! The main colony construction continued at about a 50% rate compared with before. Five years in, the schedule projection was that it would be complete in 10 more years. Overnight this changed to 20 years. The Company continued with a huge recruitment binge, scouring the globe for talent. We needed every qualified technical person we could get our hands on.

My HVAC team was huge, but we could barely keep up with the rest of construction. Nothing was manufactured on the Moon. Everything had to be fabricated dirtside and launched. All our Earth factory production was linked to our design and logistics A.I. It was just-in-time delivery to the nth degree. Fans, ducts, dampers, turning vanes, hanging rods, cable trays, maintenance platforms, embedded rock anchors, digital control systems, variable frequency drives, wiring harnesses, insulation, LED light banks, CO_2 scrubbers, humidifiers, LOTS of cables, circuit breakers, motor controllers, sound attenuation, every nut and bolt, every square meter of stainless sheet steel had to be planned and shipped. It had to unload at the colony landing pad, go through quarantine and disinfection, ship overland to the site, and transport down the tunnel to be offloaded and staged for installation. We had lots of robots to help us, but it was still a hugely labor-intensive operation for men and women working in zoot suits. Just managing the staging area at the tunnel outlet required 28 full-time staff—all in pressure suits.

The day finally came after seven years when we were ready to fully test and commission the entire system. The sealant team performed miracles, the airlocks were operational, the O2 and N were ready for release. The frozen gases were slowly released into a heating and mixing chamber, then expelled into the bitter cold of the cave. Huge radiant heating banks shone out from the walls in the path of the released, warmed gas. It was a slow, iterative process, lasting many days. Much gas refroze, and then re-melted. More was warmed and released, more refroze, more thawed. We had 20 roving teams ready with portable electric heaters, delivering 150,000 watts of electric heat to stubborn areas of air-snow. It took three weeks of 24-hour operation to fill, heat, and pressurize the cave. The recirc-fans operated in a staged fashion, moving zones of air, keeping ahead of the cold. Mofufu's insulation team had done their job flawlessly, but 50 centimeters was barely enough. The constant power input to maintain the temperature was significant. We thought we designed the solar power farm larger than necessary to give us some slack, but it was barely enough. Nevertheless, we achieved heat and pressure, with almost zero pressure drop, measured at 155 locations around the cave walls. We had air, real air, at 20 degrees C. We did it.

Releasing the ice was the final step in humidifying the cave. It was slow, but another week of 24-hour operations got it done. Since we were up to ambient air temperature, we did not need to deal with refreezing water.

The industrial-hygiene technicians certified the air was good. I stood on the loading platform at the far end of the flight cave and removed my helmet. No pressure loss, no dizziness, no blood rush to the face—everything was OK. The smell was a little stinky—a combination of welded steel and epoxy, and dust, but it was not extreme. The filtration system would take out most of it. I made a mental note to add aroma generators to the air system. Lilacs and honeysuckle would be nice, maybe vanilla and peaches too. Maybe some Middle Eastern spices? I knew a spicy Middle Easterner who could offer suggestions.

I breathed deeply. No coughing, no gasping, no choking. I felt good. I felt crazy elated. We had achieved the greatest engineering feat of the 21st century, and I was the head engineer. Sharia was on my helmet radio, watching the video feed of the grand opening. "I am SO going to fuck you!" she purred into my ear. "I am SO proud of you, baby! Hurry and get back home!" I felt like a giant and a hero and a god, all rolled in one. She always knew how to electrify me!

During flight cave construction, we had another baby, a girl named Tai-Chi. Whereas the Lunatic was 110% boy, running like a maniac most of the time, except when he hurt himself and blubbered like a baby, little Teechie was calm, serene, and quiet, with the biggest, brightest brown eyes in the known universe. Even when she hurt herself, she would just look up with those amazing eyes and a tense expression, as if to say, "Excuse me, but this is a problem!" She was also brilliant, learning to speak and walk by seven months, and wrapping two intelligent adults around her pinky finger almost daily. She even got her brother to cooperate with her schemes. He was excited to have his own pet baby sister, even though she was the one running things. We again had Sharia stay on Earth for the birth, and for Teechie's first year of life. Then they returned to the Moon, flying the geriatric flight. Teechie was fussed over by seven cooing great-grannies on the flight.

On Earth, the Company had run a raffle, with the ten winners given free trips to the Moon, free instruction in flying, and the first chance to fly in the new cave. Over 100 copies of the winning flight systems were made, with 25 copies each of the second- and third-runner-up winners. Once we had established protocols for safety, traffic patterns, rest zones, repair shops, and all the rest, more suits would be ordered. They would be leased, and all were maintained by Company technicians. The first flights were televised worldwide—a gala, media event.

The ten raffle winners (six women, four men) went through the usual dirtside training for tourists, plus the lunar-side tourist training. This was followed by 30 days of vigorous physical training. They already had to be fit enough to pass stringent standards prior to coming, but they needed flight-specific training. They were suspended in net slings horizontally and pulled on cables attached to resistance stacks. They did fierce cardio exercises, mainly with their arms. They did yoga to gain flexibility and mobility. They ate boatloads of protein.

They did multiple VR simulations, lying prone in a VR couch, watching a HOLO-video display of a proposed flight path. They checked out in the wind tunnel. They were presented with multiple scenarios, including potential crashes with other flyers. They also needed to learn how to land without crashing. Each step of training had to be passed 100%, or they would not fly.

They were fitted up with flight suits. This required the assistance of two technicians for each flyer. They were laid belly down on a padded table and inserted into the arm and leg straps, with tails controlled by leg kicks. Their heads were held up slightly with forehead straps attached to their backs, to prevent neck fatigue and to keep them able to survey their flight paths. Then came launch day, with massive media attendance. The Company did not permit live broadcasts, in case of disaster—not good publicity if they killed one of the winners on a live worldwide video feed.

The launch platform had been designed for five launches at a time, and the first five were assisted to the edge. They looked down over 350 meters to the floor below. Then the first woman launched, shouting, "Geronimo!" She soared away, floating, slowly banking, babbling like an idiot, yelling like a kid on Christmas morning. The second, third, and fourth followed, one after the other. The fifth man, to everyone's horror, just fell off the edge, but after plummeting 100 meters, he stabilized and swooped upward dramatically. He was grinning—he had done it deliberately. This part of the video was played over and over on Earth by millions of viewers—they loved it.

The Company set up HOLO-TV viewing stations in over 2,000 locations around the globe in member countries, showing the entire flight cave at times, zooming in on individual flyers at other times, and constantly panning the kiosks, equipment, facilities, and spectators (we had comfortable viewing galleries that could accommodate 300). It was a massive advertising campaign. They began to sell flight subscriptions, flight coupons, personalized flying suits, and a new clothing line. Only the filthy rich could afford to come to the Moon to fly, but people dreamed. Follow-up raffles were scheduled and run.

PART THREE: LUXURY AND BABIES

Construction resources were diverted back to the Troll Cave, with emphasis on luxury condominiums, shops, clinics, and salons. Lunar gravity was kind to aging faces—they did not sag. Breasts did not sag (Sharia was a spectacular example of this). Nothing but the best for our wealthy clientele. The Moon was changing from a science colony to a playground for the rich. The old "jumping-off point for colonization of the Solar System" drivel fell by the wayside. The Company abused its funding horribly, and even with many paid-for politicians in their pockets, they could not stop the Lunar Authority from changing the contract terms from cost-plus reimbursable to firm fixed price. Now, everything was at risk for the Company. The money spigot was tightened down considerably. The Company reduced staff, cut programs, reduced risk, and prioritized high-value activities. Moonies were being replaced with condo denizens, who added nothing to the growth of the colony except for money and demands.

No more tunnel projects. No new farm development. No new laboratories. New construction was confined to condos and a few critical systems. Maintenance continued but was strictly controlled and prioritized.

Service and security staff increased. Moonies who used to complain bitterly about how bad it was to live on the Moon suddenly talked nostalgically about the good old days. Many of the new occupants of the underground colony were decent enough folks, but there was a definite "us vs. them" attitude among the old-time Moonies.

The smarter and better newbies did their best to engage and respect us. A few of the best even came up with some damned good ideas for expanding and improving the colony at reasonable cost. Some were, after all, high-powered business entrepreneurs who were movers and shakers on Earth. They realized the need to become contributors to the Lunar community, and they integrated with aplomb. The less decent ones became resentful and demanding—they had paid for services, fair and square, dammit! They should get what they paid for! It seemed these had a perverse attraction to being publicly shunned.

The Company continued to cut costs, which meant cutting staff. Long gone were the slush personnel, only there to provide billable hours per contract. Quarterly EVMS audits were a thing of the past, as were many HR policies. Construction staff were still needed for some years, but were reduced by 60%. OT was shut off, and people who broke the rules did not get to come back as before.

The one bright spot was babies. Within six years of the birth of Tai-Chi, there were four more babies in the colony. Four more years, and there were 32 children, including ours. Mofufu and Fang had twin girls, and they were shockingly bright, cute, and pretty. The newspapers on Earth referred to it as the Moon Boom. Plenty of boom-boom going on up on the Moon! Sharia handed off her farming work to others and started the Moonbeam Academy. It is possible we had the smartest population of children in all human history.

Grades K−12 were taught by PhDs. We created a music club, physical education and competitive sports, and community engagement for the kids with our elders— the works. Every child was required to be fluent in two foreign languages upon graduation. Some spoke as many as six. We had the top educational psychologists in the world come up for sabbaticals to train our teaching staff. The kids took off like rockets. Discipline was maintained with peer involvement and parental participation.

We had visitors from the best universities on Earth, seeking to recruit our students. The typical age for graduation from grade 12 was 13. Our kids were brilliant. Some graduated at 10 or 11. Two were done at age eight. Soon, satellite university campuses were set up, and we had college for our skinny little overachievers.

Even my security buddy, Tommy Washington, got married. Anastasia was a tall, slender, stacked, stunningly beautiful Ukrainian redhead with flashing green eyes, who was one of the top escorts. I do not know how he convinced her to give up her line of work, but she truly loved him. Maybe because he was tall, handsome, powerfully built, smart, and treated her like a treasure. They were a striking and attractive pair. She was also a trained IT professional with a master's degree and a penchant for elite-level hacking. She fit in perfectly with the lunar program and culture, providing us with much-needed expertise and exquisite personal charm. On the rare occasion when I spoke personally with Anastasia and Sharia was around, I could feel her eyes burning laser beams into the back of my head, even though she was scrupulously discreet. I am not stupid—I did not want to be fed to the pigs. I also did not want Tommy to snap my spine.

I continued in my construction-engineering position but focused on the colony and not the flight cave. Sharia and I and our two miniatures went back to Earth at the same time for R&R rotation. We visited family, went to great national parks, lollygagged on the beach, and loved each other. I helped with teaching during our Earth year. The kids complained bitterly about the heavy gravity, but they always pulled through. Their bodies needed one full G. We taught them to swim, ride horses, shoot, and play Monopoly. They became expert poker players, especially Teechie. I played her a few times and lost every time. I swear she was telepathic, looking at me with those deep, solemn, brown eyes. By age 10, Tycho was winning chess matches against masters as often as he lost.

PART FOUR: NEW LAND

With the flight cave, the Moon finally became self-sustaining financially. No one dared to tally up the total cost of establishing the Lunar Colony. No one had the suicidal political inclination to do so. It was just too vast. Was it as much as $25 trillion, $50 trillion? Could those trillions have been used to clean up the Earth? Yep. But the program was in the hands of the Lunar Authority and the Company from the beginning, and they did a superb job of covering and obfuscating. There were scandals and jail sentences for a few obvious malefactors, but the money was spent and gone, never to be recovered.

The Lunar Colony was able to survive on its own, with farming and water production, retirement and rehabilitation services, medical treatments and surgeries, drug and nanoelectronics development, and the all-important flight vacation packages. The super-wealthy took a shine to the Moon, and their largesse kept us going. The farm kept us fed very well, and the Sun gave us power. Ice gave us water, oxygen, and rocket fuel.

The Moonies who complained the most eventually left permanently for Earth. I read somewhere that 17% of returned, disgruntled Moonies committed suicide within three years of dirtside return. The ones who stayed learned to accept our condo denizens. We eventually negotiated a buyout of the Company (assisted ably by those same legally astute denizens). It had been losing profit for years, and the Moon just wasn't as profitable a place as it once was. We were self-sufficient, but we did not need the Company leeches to suck off our rewards. We offered them a way out. Prior to making our offer, we co-opted the security police and brought them into our scheme (I was the link, and Tommy was my co-conspirator). We could either revolt and basically take everything they had (come and get it, if you want it!), or they could gracefully agree to terms and move on. They agreed to the terms. We formed the Lunar Holding Company, along with the Moon Bank, and we became a functioning world economy.

Moonies held citizenship in 42 countries. The illegality of what we executed was certainly held in those countries, as well as in the U.N., but who would enforce the rights of the multinational, supra-legal, predatory Company? The Company certainly had plenty of lawyers, but the U.N. ignored them. The Lunar Authority was dismantled after the buyout of the Company, so who would investigate or enforce it? It was a transnational mess for the U.N., and they decided not to decide.

Everyone on Earth knew the corruption—no one shed a tear for the Company's losses. The yacht owners had sucked off enough gravy. Many member countries benefited from the peel-off technology of lunar scientists, and they wanted to continue trade with us. By taking the Company middleman out of the way, we could sell at lower prices and still make money for the colony. But what now to call the colony? We were independent by economic declaration, and by the de facto acquiescence of member states. What were we?

We could not practically claim the entirety of the Lunar surface and subsurface. The satellite had 2.6 times the land area of the United States of America, and less than 3/100,000 the population. We were the smallest nation in existence at 1,444 citizens. We did not even know what a citizen was, or even if we wanted to have citizenship. Thus far, every child born to Moonie parents had been born on Earth in one of the member states that were originally in the Lunar Charter of 2050. Through how many generations did citizenship laws apply for people born outside their home countries?

By consensus (not mine), I was thrust into the middle of the discussion and given the title of Constitutional Recorder. My job was to assemble the laws, traditions, treaties, and declarations that went into forming a new country. I did not want to do it. Sharia was thrilled about it. Teechie told me very nonchalantly that I was the best one for the job. I looked daggers at her sweet, smiling face.

"I hate bureaucracy!" I fumed to Sharia for the fifth or twelfth time.

"Which is why you are ideal for the job," she calmly replied with flawless logic. "You have a chance that almost no man in history has had, or if he had it, was the wrong man for it. You are not Vladimir Ilyich Lenin. You are not Adolf Hitler. You are not Ayatollah Khomeini. You have no agenda, no malign ideology, no evil dreams of power. You are a brilliant engineer, Dr. Lopez, perhaps the best engineer in the Solar System. You solve problems. You invent clever new designs. You make it work efficiently. So, I see no conflict here. The only conflict is your resistance to reality and wisdom." Then she went back to preparing dinner (did I mention she is a splendid cook? Note to all men: marry the girl who raises the beets and the chickens).

Dammit. Who did this woman think she was? She was a brilliant and dynamic lady, dedicated to loving me fiercely. I had no reasonable counters. So, I gave in. It is best to quit when you are clearly beaten than to keep resisting and get truly and royally trashed. I grabbed her and kissed her, and told her, "Wait until I get you naked!" She smiled and wiggled her buns.

"Here, taste this," she offered a spoon of gravy, "Does it need any rosemary?"

"It's delicious, but not nearly as delicious as YOU."

"Flatterer!"

It took me nearly a year to assemble, review, add to, delete from, reword, and collate all the documents that I felt applied to national birthing. I read the U.S.

Constitution, the Declaration of Independence, the Magna Carta, the constitutions of Russia (the one they had before Russia dissolved into seven smaller states after the Ukraine war debacle), France, Iraq, and Thailand. I read the Meditations of Marcus Aurelius. I read court cases and legal precedents on citizenship and national identity. I read them again and again. I read the Code of Hammurabi. I read the Torah and the Koran. I read The Peloponnesian War by Thucydides. I read Machiavelli's The Prince and Greene's The Laws of Power. I read the Napoleonic law from Louisiana. I read the Constitution of the Confederate States of America. I read Wealth of Nations. I read Das Kapital and Mein Kampf, and Mao's Little Red Book. I read the Lunar Charter of 2050. I had no idea that becoming a country was so complicated, and I resolved to uncomplicate it.

For so many years, we had been controlled by the Company contract. Policies were agreed to and obeyed, not created. The one real consequence for noncompliance was deportation back to Earth. We never had any murders or rapes, or larceny. We had no pedophilia, very little assault and battery, and no libel. It is not that the cantankerous Moonies did not try, and in many cases succeeded in some of these, but the security team always handled them, and the Company used its policies to punish them.

One terrible criminal case involved a gay couple. The dominant one became abusive and began to beat and whip his partner. In public, they were professional and competent. In private, they became a building crisis. Insane jealousy and extreme demands for humiliating obedience were in the horrid mix. The sad culmination came when the submissive committed suicide. We found whip welts and bite marks on his body. His grief, depression, and hopelessness overtook him and killed him. His abuser was arrested, and we set up a trial. Everyone on the Moon knew the situation, so jury selection had to be flexible. We employed a retired civil law judge, who ran the divorce court for a county in Iowa. We had both defense and prosecution attorneys.

At the end, he was found guilty of manslaughter, sexual humiliation, assault and battery, and rape. The suicide victim had left a long and detailed account of the abuses behind, supported by photos. He called specific locations and times that provided evidence at the trial. We left the perp in lockup until we figured out what to do with him. He stayed incarcerated for three weeks, all the time cursing and taunting the guards, throwing feces at them, and attacking them when he was fed. He scratched his face and made it bleed.

And then he was gone. We checked audio and video footage of his cell and the surrounding areas. No evidence of escape or foul play. We checked the video of the hatches to the outside—nothing. There was not a spot of blood. No biological material of any kind was found, not even an eyelash. He was just gone. I asked Tommy if he knew what had happened. His face was bland and expressionless. "He just disappeared, Jeremy. That's it." I decided not to press the issue further. I could guess, but I kept it to myself, as did many others who knew what happened. There was no family on Earth to send condolences to. He was a lone, malignant narcissist. No one shed any tears.

I went to Manny Lieberman, a former corporate lawyer from New York, who had worked both as a senior contracts manager for his corporation and also clerked in the U.S. Supreme Court in his younger days. He was as sharp as any of the new retirees I met, and none of them were dumb. I asked him to review my work. "You wanna become a lawyer, Jeremy?" he asked. "You did great work here."

"No, I don't want to become a lawyer. I want to get this job done, but thanks for the compliment." Manny offered some smart edits, as well as suggesting a few more documents to add to my reading list. I then took it to Martha Choi, a retired political science professor and investor from Taiwan. She gave excellent criticism and sent me on my way. The Moon was extremely fortunate to have attracted the best and brightest that Earth had to offer.

I offered my summary and conclusions to the Steering Committee. It was made up of 19 men and women, including 4 retirees. Here are some of my questions:

1. What is a Moonie? Perhaps a Moonie is someone who has spent at least one full Earth year on the

Moon. This is the simplest way to determine eligibility for citizenship. If you come here and stay long enough, you are one of us, regardless of the reason for your arrival. You decide if you want to stay, you decide if you want to leave. Do we screen new arrivals for suitability before allowing them to stay? What criteria do we use for screening? What is the upper limit of the number of people we are willing to add?

2. What rights does a Moonie have? How can these be taken away? What felony crimes cause them to be taken away and why? Rights need to be specified only if there is a government or a court that can infringe on them. The American Bill of Rights may be a good starting point.

3. What government should we have? We are a closed system to a great degree, and our ability to expand is extremely limited. Perhaps pure democracy, with a representative council to put forward referendums?

4. Do we merge the economic corporation with the government? Is there a minimum amount of money that a new arrival must invest in the corporation in order to become a Moonie? Do we offer banking and financial services on the Moon? What about on Earth? How do we do money transfers safely and securely?

5. Do we prepare for military conflict? What potential threats do we face, and what weapons are at our disposal, or could be at our disposal? Who

commands military operations? Two or three nuclear weapons striking the colony would destroy all our surface infrastructure. Hit the 144 light shafts to the farm with one, and the blast and radiation would wipe out much of the underground colony. Do we need an aggressive missile defense system? What about invasion? How do we defeat an overwhelming, heavily armed force with civilians? Military defense is extremely expensive, and most of the technology would need to be shipped from Earth. How do we ship it in a clandestine fashion?

6. Do we set up a Department of state for diplomatic communication with nations on Earth? Would we need embassies in their countries? What is the name of our country? Should we attempt to join the U.N.?

7. What is illegal? How do we define it, and what laws are made to punish it? How are these enforced? The need for some kind of government was made painfully clear by the gay abuse case. Our ad-hoc court was OK, but we needed better in the future, for less obvious cases.

8. How big is our claimed, sovereign territory? Do we want the right to annex and develop more Lunar land? The original colony covered about 35.5 hectares, plus the land/launch complex with maintenance and refueling, plus the solar farm, maybe 95 or 96 hectares total. The shaft leading to the Troll Cave, with lifts and staging areas, covers

maybe 3 hectares. The new solar farm is another 17 hectares. The road from the original colony to the Troll Cave (yes, the Company built a road with cost-plus funding) covers 66 hectares. Everything else, except for the atrium shafts covering about 1.5 hectares, is underground. We pegged a proposed area of 10,000 square kilometers of the Lunar South Pole to begin discussion. This would make us bigger than Bahrain but smaller than Qatar.

9. Even if we wanted to expand, how do we fund expansion? How do we contract with entities on Earth to provide materials and send launches? How do we protect our legal and economic interests when dealing with said entities?

10. What types of economically viable manufacturing can we set up and run? Can we build heavy industry, such as metal refining and smelting? Can we ship our heavy material products to Earth and make a profit? What about mineral rights for areas beyond our borders?

11. How do we prevent overthrow by radical, internal forces? How do we balance personal liberty and freedom of speech and assembly with state security and public health? How do we manage police brutality?

Earthlings had no love lost for the predatory, corrupt Company, but they also did not care a fig for us. My unfortunate conversation with my friend Tyler told me there was a lot of seething resentment toward us. The general view was that we were overprivileged, arrogant, overpriced, useless leeches. These were the better attitudes. Many advocated we be attacked and conquered and "taught a lesson." What lesson we were to learn, I do not know. What they would do after conquering us is anyone's guess. Most of these ideas came from fringe people, but politicians on Earth thrived on bigotry and the sense of aggrieved victimhood. Why not blame those damned Moonies for sucking away so much money needed by the needy of Earth? No matter that it was the Lunar Authority, chartered by the U.N., working through the agency of the Company that created our colony. Facts do not matter to the ignorant and greedy. Nevertheless, this was reality—ignorance and greed make people do crazy things. We would need to defend ourselves.

In the meantime, while I was busy writing world history, we elected a 9-person ruling council, which rotated every four years—no career politicians. Service was mandatory. If you were nominated with at least 100 signatures, you could not back out except for health reasons, which basically did not exist. It was handled the same way as jury duty. We eliminated the security contract and created our own police force. The security system evolved into one overseen by the Colony (Territory? Republic? State?) rather than the Company, and we had a sheriff with four deputies democratically elected to run it, along with a chief justice, associate justice, and legal secretaries to rule the court. We established a committee to write laws and to define government-guaranteed and protected rights, and I was made the committee head. Sharia was pleased.

Part Five: Development

We expanded our adult recreation facilities. Lunar fitness training became a major pastime, with some of the best experts on Earth consulting. We were their laboratory. The goal was to mitigate the effects of low gravity on human health. Bone density loss and muscle wastage were a concern, and our scientists developed drugs and employed nutritional supplementation and genetic engineering to mitigate them. The cumulative effects of radiation exposure were monitored rigorously. Cardiovascular systems became sluggish unless regularly stressed. The biggest push in our pharmaceutical research laboratories was not curing diseases on Earth, but making humans adapt better to the Moon. Stem cell therapies, hypobaric oxygen, platelet-rich plasma, gene editing, and red-light therapy were big, as were other viable life extension therapies.

We took fewer trips dirtside. The cost was extreme, and the colony was not yet profitable, standing on its own. It was not law, but everyone knew they needed to maintain the tough workout schedule of two hours a day. It was simple common sense. We were, for all practical purposes, creating a new human species, Homo Lunaris.

We continued to maintain ferocious quarantine regulations and enforcement, but despite these, disease occasionally reared its head. Some got sick and got better. Some were medevac'd back to Earth. We needed some bacteria and viruses just to maintain our bodily defenses, but it was a tightrope walk. Any outbreak could devastate the entire colony in no time—we were a closed system. Infractions against public health were treated as high crimes. No anti-vax nonsense on the Moon. Genetic engineering for disease resistance was a top priority in our labs.

Sharia and I had more kids. Five more kids: Toby, Tanya, Taser, Thomas, and Titania. There was plenty of expansion room in the cave, and our family home became a rabbit warren. Tycho attended the University of Chicago and then McGill in Montreal. He stayed on Earth, found a gorgeous girl in Canada to marry, and they settled down in Alberta. Tai-Chi became a medical doctor at age 17 and went into medical research back on the Moon.

By the year 2105, we were an independent nation—South Pole Moon—applying for membership in the U.N. Then disaster struck, followed by an even greater disaster.

CRASH

PART ONE: STRANDED

The asteroid that hit the old colony surface facility was ten times the size of a refrigerator and traveling at 74,000 KPH. The impact force was roughly 1.8 kilotons. While no one was inside the surface modules at the time, the explosion cut off all communication and support for the launch/landing area. The lander maintenance sheds were severely damaged, so no refit/repair operations could take place, not even basic maintenance. Suddenly, the entire colony was stranded. The Achilles' heel of the colony was our lifeline with Earth. Now it was cut.

We contacted several agencies on Earth for assistance. We had plenty of money in the bank—we could pay for supplies to make repairs. We had all the technical expertise to accomplish it. One after another, various agencies and governments gave us neutral responses, ranging from "we will give this question some study" to "we do not have resources available" to "we have no formal trade agreements with you" to "you are not a recognized state." No one cared about the overpaid, arrogant Moonies.

We were baffled. We thought we had good relations with many suppliers, contractors, and agencies, as well as with several foreign governments. This nonresponse from nearly every one of them made no sense. Something had to be behind it. We got in touch with as many of our trusted agents as we could to have them investigate behind the scenes, to reach out to counterparts, and to get a sense of the pulse. What they told us was not good. "We got the cold shoulder. People are scared to talk. Some who were once friendly are now hostile." We told our people to lie low and keep a low level of general surveillance.

PART TWO: SUPPLIES

There was no immediate impact from the loss of shipments from Earth. We were self-sufficient in most basic commodities—food, electricity, oxygen. The one thing that would slow down soon was ice mining. We needed carbide cutting teeth for the rock cutters and borers. We needed a steady supply of lubricants and replacement parts. We had logistics agents back dirtside who did a superb job of accessing supplies and getting them to us without paying exorbitant prices. Most suppliers, when they heard something was for the lunar colony, automatically increased prices by 30–40%. They knew they had us by the throat, so they charged as much as they could get away with. Our agents set up shell companies, with multiple intermodal operations under holding companies spanning six continents, to launder the supplies. Most suppliers did not know the intended destination, so the prices were more competitive. Our excellent retirees helped us with the organization and execution of our logistics strategy. Manny Lieberman became the go-to guy for this. Martha Choi was his deputy. He was an encyclopedia of legal knowledge about corporations. He knew port fees, tariffs, logistics contracts, and service agreements. He helped shepherd us— technically brilliant but business-stupid Moonies— through the maze and maelstrom of international commerce and trade.

"I can do this shit in my sleep, Jeremy!" he chortled to me one day. "I'm having a gas! I haven't had this much fun since we took down our main competitor with an antitrust suit! Those bastards hated my guts!"

For the next 14 months, we managed to get about 55% of the supplies we needed. Getting lift capacity was the worst—we were charged $1,250 per kilogram, five times the normal commercial rate. The suppliers had to send disposable gear capsules to us—we could not operate our launch facility. Our second toughest hurdle was guaranteeing payment for our products and services. Manny helped with the shell companies, the LLCs, and the legal cover to keep us hidden. It was as if a virulent virus of hatred for Moonies had settled over the entire planet.

Getting weapons was very, very tough. Tommy was a great help in suggesting the best alternatives, plus there was a huge list of possible options. In addition to high-velocity rifles with ballistic computer-aided scopes, we managed to score some shoulder-fired lasers—450-kilowatt jobs that could burn through 25 millimeters of AR500 steel armor plate in about a quarter second. We got explosives, we got knives, we got anti-missile systems, we got low-horizon tracking radars. We wanted nuclear weapons, but we were stymied. Luckily, if they nuked us, being hundreds of meters below solid rock was a huge advantage—with the exception of the light wells and the entry ramp.

Accurate hits in either of these areas would not obliterate us, but they would be horribly damaging.

We had crews repairing the launch facility, but it was slow going. We could not call up Uncle Company to send us everything our hearts desired. We held civil defense drills and first aid training. Tommy put me in charge of marksmanship training. At first, I resisted, thinking I was unqualified. Tommy would have none of it. "Jeremy, stop being stupid! You learned how to shoot when you were 6 years old, for Christ's sake! I've seen your range groups, and you consistently shoot at 0.25 MOA. What the fuck, bro'?"

We scored some amazing hardware. By some miracle, we acquired a surplus GAU-8 Avenger Gatling gun with 2,300 rounds of 30mm armor-piercing ammunition. Add optics up to 150x power plus infrared and night vision. Firing at a thousand meters per second, I could hit targets very accurately on the lunar surface at distances above 8 kilometers. No windage, no humidity, very little bullet drop. Not even any Coriolis to account for. About 10% of the rounds consistently hit 0.5 MOA, plus or minus 40 meters at 8 kilometers. This is more than adequate for anti-materiel shots. The toughest part of shooting outside was manipulating my zoot suit and not damaging anything. We set it up in a location near the likely landing zone, using a slick, huge tripod rigged up by our engineers in the machine shop. This worked.

By another miracle, we were able to obtain two SKYBURN systems—50,000-kilowatt, radar-guided lasers for anti-missile defense, made by the United Kingdom. These were huge units, weighing over 20 tons each. How we were able to get them approved by the U.K. Foreign Ministry, I will never know. It appears some of our smart retirees had friends in very high places, and many strings were pulled and favors called in. Lots of money was paid, too. I think a lot of the U.K. FM staff were sympathetic to the lunar cause.

We got our anti-missile hardware from Ukraine. They were amazingly supportive, relative to the rest of the world. They suffered through four years of grueling combat with the Russians and took more than 30 years to rebuild after the war. They knew an underdog when they saw one, and they knew the power of hate propaganda. They were also a big part of what drove the Iranians into the Treaty of Ankara. After defeating Russia, Ukraine went on a mission to sink Iranian-flagged vessels, due to Tehran's help with bomb drones to the Russians. Note to self: do not fuck with the Ukrainians. The treaty not only re-established diplomatic relations with the United States, but it also established reparations for Ukraine.

Another country that was helpful to us was Hong Kong. After the downfall of the Chinese Communist Party in 2035 and the breakup of China into multiple mafia-tong fiefdoms, HK came out as a sovereign nation. The United Kingdom had a strong hand in helping them.

Their extensive banking and business connections made it possible for us to get things done dirtside. It did not hurt that Manny had visited on business over a dozen times in his career and spoke passable Chinese. Our main shell business, HK Holdings, was based there. You want to get something done fast and quietly? Call on the Hong Kong Chinese. Manny drafted Fang to help him.

Who else helped us? The heavy-lift rocket companies. During the heyday of the Company, they made money in bushel baskets full. It has been steadily dying down since we became independent. With us not only trying to build long-term stocks of everything, but also adding weapons and other valuables to the mix. We paid well, so we gave them a new lease on life. Further, we planned to expand, to build a second launch facility, and start new ice mines. Our plans stretched into the future for many years, and they were happy to be on board with us.

The U.N., however, did not love us. They felt cheated, robbed, bamboozled. They invoked the U.N. Lunar Charter of 2050. It laid out lunar sovereignty being granted by the U.N. So, if the U.N. giveth, then the U.N. can taketh away—or so they reasoned. I was gently coerced by my family and friends to draft a Declaration of Independence. In my spare time, I was to draft the Lunar Constitution. I press-ganged Manny Lieberman and Martha Choi to help. Instead of building on the

American template, strong though that was, we decided to chart our own course.

Our foundational argument was simple: while the U.N. may have acknowledged our sovereignty, we said this was a simple statement of fact. A people can determine their own sovereignty, and no one can take it away. The U.S. Declaration of Independence was clear on this principle.

U.N. officials made rumblings about seizing our assets, but we had done such an incredible job of hiding them and playing a shell company game, they did not know where to begin. None of our employees were directly employed by us, or even by shell companies. Our money transactions were laundered through 120 outlets, then re-laundered through 800 more outlets. Money in and money out was treated the same—as invisible, but completely effective for suppliers and contractors. Yes, we had to pay a hell of a lot in fees, but it protected us completely.

Despite our good friends and helpers, the general population hated us. We were no longer taking any money for support—the blockchain program was severely truncated to only cover UBI payments—but even this was somehow our fault. We existed—this was our crime. I have no doubt that many good things could have been done with those trillions of dollars, but even under the Company's greedy stewardship, we had been the biggest stimulant to the world economy for decades. Even in our reduced circumstances, we were still a very large economic benefit to hundreds of industries around the world.

Nevertheless, with the severe reduction in our scope of needs, this threw many people out of good-paying jobs and back onto UBI, which was a de facto prison sentence. The dirtside jingle was "UBI 'till you die." Our fault, of course. We offered to set up training centers to teach high-end technical skills, but were rebuffed by most (not the Ukrainians, nor the Hong Kongers).

We offered mining contracts with the major mining players for mining rare earth and other metals—the Moon had them in abundance. They refused our terms—we insisted on retaining sovereignty and control over security, transport, and profits. We allowed reasonable profits, as well as reasonable pricing terms. No go. They were greedy. We countered with an offer of significant technical support (we had been mining the Moon for over 40 years). They knew better—they were the experts and did not need our help. Good luck with learning all the hard lessons from scratch. It was a dirty shame—partnering with the likes of Rio Tinto and Barrick would have opened immense new metals markets and provided many needed rare earths to the world economy. After the breakup of China and the downfall of the CCP, exports of rare earths had dropped.

PART THREE: ATTACK

Despite having read as much history as I have, it never ceases to amaze me how stupid governments can be. I am certain that, for millennia, politicians were the same — just in it for position, popularity, and power. Some of the main instigators were the Turks and the Brazilians, supported by the reconstructed South African Federation. Myanmar, Hungary, and Ecuador were in the game, too. But the surprise (at least for me) was that the United States was leading the charge to "take control of the Moon" and to "get our money's worth out of those thieves." Somehow, I still thought the U.S. had some decency and common sense. I was wrong.

I continue to be dazzled by the incompetence of many military adventures. The Russian invasion of Ukraine, the American intervention in Iraq, and Napoleon's march into Moscow are all examples of things going sideways and then south, very fast. Most generals fight according to the rules of the most recent war. Most soldiers are not trained for new environments. The Moon is a VERY bad place for on-the-job training for an invasion force. Forget deserts. Forget mountains. Forget jungles. The Moon is orders of magnitude harder. Daylight surface temperatures are 120 °C. It is incredibly easy to tear a hole in a pressure suit, and then goodbye. You are done.

The silly dirtside armchair warriors thought the low gravity would make it easy. They assumed an overwhelming force could be applied. They had no clue what and how many weapons we had (a lot — even years after the First Lunar War ended, it is still a state secret). They thought we hid inside our caves all the time, and they could simply close off all entrances and exits and wait for our surrender. Oh no, boys and girls. Not Moonies. We had learned that we loved freedom and financial independence and a functioning economy way too much to allow some grasping, grievance-fueled dirtbags to take it from us.

The United States government was stupid enough to give us an ultimatum and a deadline. They gave us four weeks, which meant they had been assembling and training their invasion force already. They had probably been recruiting for at least a year. We learned later that the instigating governments offered huge financial incentives to volunteers. It meant they would be ready for their first launch in three weeks. We prepared accordingly.

Tommy and I were joined by six other Moonies with military experience (one was an actual retired general — French Foreign Legion), and we became the general staff. We gamed it out with the aid of artificial intelligence — how would WE conduct an invasion? We assumed they would have few surface vehicles, so a foot march was the likely method to approach us. There is only so much a soldier can carry, even in 1/6-

G. They would likely take control of our launch facility and try to blot out all communications. They might try to gas us. I have no doubt they were prepared to kill as many of us as needed, and then enslave the rest, under the fiction of "re-employment." We were to be taught a lesson we would never forget. It was pure ethnic hatred, with the ethnicity of Moonie being the target of hatred. Creating a subhuman group to blame for society's ills is tried-and-true. We were despicable because we existed.

PART FOUR: ONE DAY

WAR

For outside duty we set up four rotating six-hour shifts. Six hours may not seem long, but sitting still and quiet, doing nothing but watching a dead world is not easy. We needed every soldier to be alert. We set up eight squads of 16 outsiders in eight strategic locations. Many of my beam-team veterans volunteered, along with some of Mofufu's insulating crew — they had the most zoot-suit experience. Radar was manned 24/7. All radio and video transmissions, as well as any news from the Earth, were watched and analyzed. It paid off.

They sent a fleet of 24 vessels — 20 troop transports with 20 soldiers each, and four supply transports with food, water, weapons, and extra pressure suits. They thought they could sneak-attack, doing a lunar orbital insertion 180 degrees around the globe from us, followed by a half orbit to come to the colony and land. One group was to take the launch facility without damaging it. One group was to commandeer the tunnel to the Troll Cave. One group was to set up communications and electronic countermeasures. They failed as spectacularly as the Russian invasion of Ukraine in 2022. They thought we were unarmed, with no military to speak of.

I was doing surface duty when we got the call, "They're on the way! Arrival in 15 minutes." They came on schedule. I was manning the GAU-8 when the first troop lander slowed and descended. I punched a bunch of holes through it. A three-second burst yielded about 200 rounds (I remember Tommy ordering me to use only quick bursts. "I will break your goddamn neck if you don't," he admonished). I assumed everyone inside was suited up, so maybe there were no casualties yet. They should be so lucky. I fired at the engine, and it burst into flames. Twenty dead soldiers. I was way keyed up and full of adrenaline, but I still reported to Tommy. I heard his deep, Trinidad/Texas accent: "Good boy, Jeremy!" Calls were coming in from other defenders. A supply ship was shot down with the SKYBURN laser. Two more troop ships exploded by two more SKYBURNS. Four more troop ships with multiple holes managed to land. Once they landed, my 30mm fire was unrelenting, making the landers into Swiss cheese. One supply ship managed to land unhurt, and we sent a squad of sixteen to take it from the dirtbags. Two troop ships landed unhurt, and soldiers disembarked. The remaining transports aborted their landings and returned to orbit.

One of our technicians who used to work for Mofufu had a shoulder-fired laser, and he began to burn dirtbags. The troops from the two landers were hampered by their inability to walk or move efficiently in low gravity. They kicked up clouds of dust. Their headlamps were visible for two thousand meters. It was a turkey shoot. No one can see a laser when it fires; they did not know what direction the shots came from. All died.

"Jeremy, go help the guys who are guarding the captured transport," Tommy ordered. By common consensus, Tommy was our Combat Commander. "I am on my way!" I bounced over to the transport and one of our guys gestured for me to go inside. There were several unsuited, dead Earthlings in it. Their skin was gray and flaccid. Vacuum is hard on a human body. That was not the news. The news was the four 30-kt nuclear warheads. These were each designed to be toted in two huge backpacks by two soldiers and placed like land mines. My stomach turned inside out. Before my eyes, I saw the destruction of the entire colony. I just hoped there were no more in orbit. They came with operator's manuals. They also had several heavy machine guns with ammunition, and 50 light anti-tank rocket launchers with 800 rockets.

"We need to hustle these things out of here and get them to a safe spot. Shiva, you and Tahir stay behind and rig this thing with enough explosives to blow it to bits. There is still plenty of fuel, so it should be easy." "Got it, boss!" I was thinking fast. I didn't want the Earthlings to know we had these nukes. I spoke with Tommy on an encrypted, tight-beam channel. We talked for about 20 minutes, and he got input from his brain trust of Moonies. We made a plan.

PART FIVE:
NEGOTIATIONS

We volunteered Manny to be our chief negotiator. We needed someone tough and mean, and there is no one tougher or meaner than a Jewish lawyer from New York. "Sure, Jeremy, I'll do it," he said, "Just tell me what you want me to say to these assholes." I love Manny. We had to cover up the fact that we were now a nuclear-armed state. We knew that they could not stay in orbit forever and would need to land to take on fuel for the return trip to Earth. We controlled the launch site and the fuel supply. They were forced to parley with us.

Manny was wicked right off the bat with his first words to the surviving Earth military commander. "We shot the shit out of you assholes! We blew up two supply ships, right outa of the sky, and nine troop ships! No survivors. Yeah, you heard that right. Not one dirtbag left alive." We did not tell them that one of the supply transports survived, and we had the nukes.

Silence on the other end. Manny continued, "We know you will need to land sooner or later to refuel, unless you all want to starve in orbit. Good luck with a rescue mission from home." We were pretty certain that Earth had used almost all its operational space assets to execute the invasion. Besides, the landers were not equipped or set up for orbital docking. No spacewalks on the horizon anytime soon.

"Now," continued our fiendish attorney, "Do you want to go home, or not? It's entirely up to you. We'll wait for your reply. Take your time!" I was glad that I had never been cross-examined by Manny. The acting commander, a man with a Russian accent, finally answered. "What do you suggest?"

"Now you listen up real good, Ivan," Manny pronounced it "EYE-van," like a smart-assed New Yorker. Manny continued with a gloat in his voice, "We are gonna give you a location where you may land peaceably. You may ONLY land in our prescribed location, AND at the prescribed time. If you deviate by one kilometer or one hour, we will blow you out of the sky. Sound like a plan?" I was also glad I never sat across a conference table from Manny in a negotiation.

"How do I know you will not trick us and attack us when we descend?" Ivan was suspicious of us. "You have only my word and nothing else," said Manny. "What? You're gonna orbit for 100 years to debate it? This is your ONLY option for getting out of this alive."

"We agree," Ivan replied. "I must communicate with our headquarters. Please give us one hour, and we will be ready to listen to your instructions." "No sweat, Ivan, but do not think for one second that you can gain any foothold here without our generous cooperation. Do NOT let your stupid masters back on Earth try to talk you into anything foolish. You're not suicidal, are you?" "Understood" was all that came back. "OK, one hour, starting NOW."

Fortunately, we had a lunar rover that could handle cargo and make decent speed. We hauled one of the nukes out 20 kilometers from the colony. It could be detonated remotely by radio signal — it was all in the instructions, including what frequency to use. The prescribed landing area was within a 200-meter radius of the bomb. We hid it with rocks and then pulled back to base.

It appeared that Ivan was able to talk sense into his masters, because after an hour, he agreed to our terms. It took them a couple of orbits at two hours each to get everyone landed. "Keep everyone inside!" Manny ordered. "Only Ivan comes out, so we can have a nice little chat. We have plenty of firepower trained on your vessels, so just tell everyone to be patient and sit tight. You all MIGHT survive this little party."

We let Manny continue to roll, after Ivan (his actual name, it turned out, pronounced "ee-VAHN") came into the colony under Tommy's armed guard. "Here are our terms," Manny started:

1. Empty out your cargo transports. We confiscate and take as war prizes all your materiel. We also keep the transport. "Do you have any unusual or special weapons on any of your ships?" Manny asked. "Yes, we had nuclear warheads, but they

were destroyed by your attack," replied Ivan. Checkmark that box. Smart Manny! Manny gave Ivan a long, stone-cold look. "Goddamn NUKES?" was all he said after a full minute of staring.

2. "You are allowed to keep food and water only. All weapons and other items of interest remain here with us."

3. "We will assist you with transporting LOX and LH2 to refuel your tanks. You will provide two people per lander to work with us, and we will oversee the transfer under armed guard. NO ONE will take off without our express permission. You go when we say you can go."

4. "We have four nuclear warheads, 30-kt each." Ivan's face showed shock at this. Again, Manny paused for a pregnant minute. "We have the technology to deliver them to any point on Earth. It is much easier for us to launch a missile down your gravity well than for you to launch one up out of it. We're thinking Washington, D.C. would be a nice place to start. Or should we try Moscow, Ivan? Before you launch, you will communicate this fact with your superiors, on a frequency that we monitor. Tell them we expect basic, respectful treatment as a sovereign nation, with U.N. membership, trade and banking agreements, and reasonable access for our citizens to visit Earth. Their passports are to be honored with no harassment when they travel. Each belligerent nation will provide a diplomat with the sole portfolio of writing these agreements. We

make no specific threats. These weapons are our insurance policy. We just want to be on an equal footing with everyone else."

5. "Tell your people in the landers that we have one of the warheads armed and ready to detonate within 200 meters of your landing sites. If you double-cross us, or attempt any military action, or launch without permission, we will detonate it as you are rising into the sky. I'll push the goddamned button myself!"

Whew! This last item gave me chills. I did not know if I could push the button for a nuclear attack. It was tough enough on my psyche to have sent a ship with 20 human beings burning to the ground. I hoped I didn't have nightmares.

Ivan stared at Manny for a long time. Then he smiled.

Ivan looked at us with respect. "Maybe I should become a Moonie. You are strong and brave people." "We can discuss all such possibilities AFTER we receive your appointed diplomats. We don't fault you for being loyal to your country. You caused no deaths and took no prizes from us. We have a screening process, and if you pass, maybe you can join us."

Thus began the Republic of Luna. We became the new Dubai, except nuclear-armed. The crazies on Earth had to swallow their bile. We kept expanding our lunar footprint, year by year. We also increased our nuclear armaments — again, insurance against the future. I was elected President and served eight years (I complained bitterly about this, but Sharia and Teechie were proud). Manny, at age 91, became our first Secretary of State. He served for 27 years until his death. He went deaf and blind but remained razor-sharp to the end.

Glory to the Moon! Glory to the Moonies!

9 781964 963761